To Ashley:

august 1988

wishing you years

of reading fun.

Love,

Aunt Kylie +

Keith.

6^{95}

Printed in Hong Kong

1 2 3 4 5 6 7 8 9 10

Library of Congress Cataloging-in-Publication Data

Yeatman, Linda
My Favorite Goodnight Stories

Summary: A collection of popular traditional tales
suitable for use as bedtime stories, including ''Jack and
the Beanstalk,'' ''The Old Woman and Her Pig,'' ''Henny Penny,''
and tales from China, Africa, and Greek and Christian legend.
1. Tales (1. folklore) I. Offen, Hilda, Ill.
II. Title. III. Title My Favorite Goodnight Stories.
PZ8.1.Y33MY 1987   398.2   86–18616

ISBN 0-671-63360-0

My favorite GOODNIGHT STORIES

Chosen and retold by Linda Yeatman
Illustrated by Hilda Offen

LITTLE SIMON
Published by Simon & Schuster, Inc., New York

Contents

Jack and the Beanstalk

Traditional English

There was once a boy called Jack. His mother thought he was lazy, and she was right. Jack did not like work, but he was brave and quick-witted, as you will see from this story. He lived with his mother in a small cottage and their most valuable possession was their cow, Milky-White. But the day came when Milky-White gave them no milk and Jack's mother said she must be sold.

"Take her to market," she told Jack, "and mind you get a good price for her."

So Jack set out to market leading Milky-White by her halter. After a while he sat down to rest by the side of the road. An old man came by and Jack told him where he was going.

"Don't bother to go to the market," the old man said. "Sell your cow to me. I will pay you well. Look at these beans. Only plant them, and overnight you will find you have the finest bean plants in all the world. You'll be better off with these beans than with an old cow or money. Now, how many is five, Jack?"

"Two in each hand and one in your mouth," replied Jack, as sharp as a needle.

"Right you are, here are five beans," said the old man and he handed the beans to Jack and took Milky-White's halter.

When he reached home, his mother said, "Back so soon, Jack? Did you get a good price for Milky-White?"

Jack told her how he had exchanged the cow for five beans and before he could finish his account, his mother started to shout and box his ears. "You lazy good-for-nothing boy," she screamed, "how could you hand over our cow for five old beans? What will we live on now? We shall starve to death, you stupid boy."

She flung the beans through the open window and sent Jack to bed without his supper.

When Jack woke the next morning there was a strange green light in his room. All he could see from the window was green leaves. A huge beanstalk had shot up overnight. It grew higher than he could see. Quickly Jack got dressed and stepped out of the window right onto the beanstalk and started to climb.

"The old man said the beans would grow overnight," he thought. "They must indeed be very special beans."

Higher and higher Jack climbed until at last he reached the top and found himself on a strange road. Jack followed it until he came to a great castle where he could smell the most delicious breakfast. Jack was hungry. It had been a long climb and he had had nothing to eat since midday the day before. Just as he reached the door of the castle he nearly tripped over the feet of an enormous woman.

"Here, boy," she called. "What are you doing? Don't you know my husband likes to eat boys for breakfast? It's lucky I have already fried up some bacon and mushrooms for him today, or I'd pop you in the frying pan. He can eat you tomorrow, though."

"Oh, please don't let him eat me," pleaded Jack. "I only came to ask you for a bite to eat. It smells so delicious."

Now the giant's wife had a kind heart and did not really enjoy cooking boys for breakfast, so she gave Jack a bacon sandwich. He was still eating it when the ground began to shake with heavy footsteps, and a loud voice boomed: "Fee, Fi, Fo, Fum."

"Quick, hide!" cried the giant's wife and she pushed Jack into the oven. "After breakfast, he'll fall asleep," she whispered. "That is when you must creep away." She left the oven door open a crack so that Jack could see into the room. Again the terrible rumbling voice came:

"Fee, Fi, Fo, Fum,
I smell the blood of an Englishman,
Be he alive or be he dead,
I'll grind his bones to make my bread."

A huge giant came into the room. "Boys, boys, I smell boys," he shouted. "Wife, have I got a boy for breakfast today?"

"No, dear," she said soothingly. "You have got bacon and mushrooms. You must still be smelling the boy you ate last week."

The giant sniffed the air suspiciously but at last sat down. He wolfed his breakfast of bacon and mushrooms, drank a great bucketful of steaming tea and crunched up a massive slice of toast. Then he fetched a couple of bags of gold from a cupboard and started counting gold coins. Before long he dropped off to sleep.

Quietly Jack crept out of the oven. Carefully he picked up two gold coins and ran as fast as he could to the top of the beanstalk. He threw the gold down to his mother's garden and climbed after it. At the bottom he found his mother looking in amazement at the gold coins and the beanstalk. Jack told her of his adventures in the giant's castle and when she examined the gold she realized he must be speaking the truth.

Jack and his mother used the gold to buy food. But the day came when the money ran out, and Jack decided to climb the beanstalk again.

It was all the same as before, the long climb, the road to the castle, the smell of breakfast and the giant's wife. But she was not so friendly this time.

"Aren't you the boy who was here before," she asked, "on the day that some gold was stolen from under my husband's nose?"

But Jack convinced her she was wrong and in time her heart softened again and she gave him some breakfast. Once more as Jack was eating the ground shuddered and the great voice boomed: "Fee, Fi, Fo, Fum." Quickly, Jack jumped into the oven.

As he entered, the giant bellowed:

"Fee, Fi, Fo, Fum,
I smell the blood of an Englishman,
Be he alive or be he dead,
I'll grind his bones to make my bread."

The giant's wife put a plate of sizzling sausages before him, telling him he must be mistaken. After breakfast the giant fetched a hen from a back room. Every time he said "Lay!" the hen laid an egg of solid gold.

"I must steal that hen, if I can," thought Jack, and he waited until the giant fell asleep. Then he slipped out of the oven, snatched up the hen and ran for the top of the beanstalk. Keeping the hen under one arm, he scrambled down as fast as he could.

Jack's mother was waiting but she was not pleased when she saw the hen.

"Another of your silly ideas, is it, bringing an old hen when you might have brought us some gold?"

Then Jack set the hen down carefully, and commanded "Lay!" just as the giant had done. To his mother's surprise the hen laid an egg of solid gold.

Jack and his mother now lived in great luxury. But in time Jack became a little bored and he made up his mind to climb the beanstalk once more.

This time he did not risk talking to the giant's wife in case she recognized him. He slipped into the kitchen when she was not looking, and hid himself in the log basket. He watched the giant's wife prepare breakfast and then he heard the giant's roar:

"Fee, Fi, Fo, Fum,
I smell the blood of an Englishman,
Be he alive or be he dead,
I'll grind his bones to make my bread."

"If it's that nervy boy who stole your gold and our magic hen, then I'll help you catch him," said the giant's wife. "Why don't we look in the oven? It's my guess he'll be hiding there."

You may be sure that Jack was glad he was not in the oven. The giant and his wife hunted high and low but never thought to look in the log basket. At last they gave up and the giant sat down to breakfast.

After he had eaten, the giant fetched a harp. When he commanded "Play!" the harp played the most beautiful music. Soon the giant fell asleep, and Jack crept out of the log basket. Quickly he snatched up the harp and ran. But the harp called out loudly, "Master, save me! Save me!" and the giant woke. With a roar of rage he chased after Jack.

Jack raced down the road toward the beanstalk with the giant's footsteps thundering behind him. When he reached the top of the beanstalk he threw down the harp and started to slither down after it. The giant followed, and now the whole beanstalk shook and shuddered with his weight, and Jack feared for his life. At last he reached the ground, and seizing an ax he chopped at the beanstalk with all his might. *Snap!*

"Look out, mother!" he called as the giant came tumbling down, head first. He lay dead at their feet with the beanstalk on the ground beside them. The harp was broken, but the hen continued to lay golden eggs for Jack and his mother and they lived happily for a long, long time.

Anansi and Common Sense

Traditional African and Caribbean

You may already know that Anansi is a spider, an impudent spider, full of tricks and surprises, but did you know that Anansi is responsible for the fact that everyone – or almost everyone – has a little bit of common sense? This is how it happened.

Anansi was feeling full of importance one day, and thought the cleverest thing he could do was to collect up all the common sense in the world and keep it safe in one place. So he scuttled here and scuttled there, gathering it up in a great calabash. He then plugged the calabash with a roll of dried leaves.

"There," he said to himself, "is all the common sense in the world. Whenever I need it I shall be able to help myself, and my enemies will have none. I *shall* have fun for I shall always get the better of them." He really was pleased with himself.

"Hey, wait a minute though," he thought, "where can I keep it safe? Everyone will want to steal it from me. I know, I'll put the calabash at the top of that great coconut tree. None of the other animals will ever find it."

So Anansi got a long rope and tied it around the calabash, and then he looped the other end of the rope around his head. The calabash hung down in front of him, leaving all his legs free to climb the tree.

Well, Anansi started to climb the tree, but it was not easy as the calabash kept bumping around between him and the trunk of the tree. Slowly he inched up on his eight legs until, suddenly, when he was about half way up, he heard laughter.

Now there is nothing Anansi hates more than being laughed at. Looking down he saw a small boy and the small boy was laughing his head off.

"Fancy climbing a tree with the calabash in front of you, Anansi!" he called out. "Surely you know that if you want to climb a tree with a calabash, it is more sensible to put the calabash on your back."

Anansi quivered with annoyance. In fact he was furious, for what the small boy said was common sense, yet hadn't he, Anansi, collected all the common sense in the world and stuffed it into the calabash?

In a rage he flung the calabash to the foot of the tree, where it shattered. The common sense inside was scattered into little pieces and blown all over the world, and everyone, or nearly everyone, got a little bit. So when you show you have some common sense, remember you have Anansi the Spider to thank for it.

Beauty and the Beast

Madame de Beaumont

A rich merchant who had three sons and three daughters lived in a big house in the city. His youngest daughter was so beautiful she was called Beauty by all who knew her. She was as sweet and good as she was beautiful. Sadly all of the merchant's ships were lost at sea and he and his family had to move to a small cottage in the country. His sons worked hard on the land and Beauty was happy working in the house, but his two elder daughters complained and grumbled all day long, especially about Beauty.

One day, news came that a ship had arrived which would make the merchant wealthy again. The merchant set off to the city, and just before he left he said, "Tell me, daughters, what gifts would you like me to bring back for you?"

The two older girls asked for fine clothes and jewels, but Beauty wanted nothing. Realizing this made her sisters look greedy, she thought it best to ask for something. "Bring me a rose, father," she said, "just a beautiful red rose."

When the merchant reached the city he found disaster had struck once more and the ship's cargo was ruined. He took the road home wondering how to break the news to his children. He was so deep in thought that he lost his way. Worse still, it started to snow, and he feared he would never reach home alive. Just as he despaired he noticed lights ahead, and riding toward them he saw a fine castle. The gates stood open and flares were alight in the courtyard. In the stables a stall stood empty with hay in the manger and clean bedding on the floor ready for his horse.

The castle itself seemed to be deserted, but a fire was burning in the dining hall where a table was laid with food. The merchant ate well, and, still finding no one, went upstairs to a bedroom which had been prepared. "It is almost as if I were expected," he thought.

In the morning he found clean clothes had been laid out for him and breakfast was on the table in the dining hall. After he had eaten he fetched his horse and as he rode away he saw a spray of red roses growing from a rose bush. Remembering Beauty's request, and thinking he would be able to bring a present for at least one daughter, he plucked a rose from the bush.

Suddenly a beastlike monster appeared. "Is this how you repay my hospitality?" it roared. "You eat my food, sleep in my guest room and then insult me by stealing my flowers. You shall die for this."

The merchant pleaded for his life, and begged to see his children once more before he died. At last the beast relented.

"I will spare your life," it said, "if one of your daughters will come here willingly and die for you. Otherwise you must promise to return within three months and die yourself."

The merchant agreed to return and went on his way. At home his children listened with sorrow to his tales of the lost cargo and his promise to the monster. His two elder daughters turned on Beauty, saying, "Your stupid request for a rose has brought all this trouble on us. It is your fault that father must die."

When the three months were up Beauty insisted on going to the castle with her father, pretending only to ride with him for company on the journey. The beast met them, and asked Beauty if she had come of her own accord, and she told him she had.

"Good," he said. "Now your father can go home and you will stay with me."

"What shall I call you?" she asked bravely.

"You may call me Beast," he replied.

Certainly he was very ugly and it seemed a good name for him. Beauty waved a sad farewell to her father. But she was happy that at least she had saved his life.

As Beauty wandered through the castle she found many lovely rooms and beautiful courtyards with gardens. At last she came to a room which was surely meant just for her. It had many of her favorite books and objects in it. On the wall hung a beautiful mirror and to her surprise, as she looked into it, she saw her father arriving back at their home and her brothers and sisters greeting him. The picture only lasted a few seconds then faded. "This Beast may be ugly, but he is certainly kind," she thought. "He gives me all the things I like and allows me to know how my family is without me."

That night at supper the Beast joined her. He sat and stared at her. At the end of the meal he asked: "Will you marry me?"

Beauty was startled by the question but said as gently as she could, "No, Beast, you are kind but I cannot marry you."

Each day it was the same. Beauty had everything she wanted during the day and each evening the Beast asked her to marry him, and she always said no.

One night Beauty dreamed that her father lay sick. She asked the Beast if she could go to him, and he refused, saying that if she left him he would die of loneliness. But when he saw how unhappy Beauty was, he said:

"If you go to your family, will you return within a week?"

"Of course," Beauty replied.

"Very well, just place this ring on your dressing table the night you wish to return, and you shall come back here. But do not stay away longer than a week, or I shall die."

The next morning Beauty awoke to find herself in her own home. Her father was indeed sick, but Beauty nursed him lovingly. Beauty's sisters were jealous once more. They thought that if she stayed at home longer than a week the Beast would kill her. So they pretended to love her and told her how much they had missed her. Before Beauty knew what had happened ten days had passed. Then she had a dream that the Beast was lying still as though he were dead by the lake near his castle.

"I must return at once," she cried and she placed her ring on the dressing table.

The next morning she found herself once more in the Beast's castle. All that day she expected to see him, but he never came. "I have killed the Beast," she cried, "I have killed him." Then she remembered that in her dream he had been by the lake and quickly she ran there. He lay still as death, down by the water's edge.

"Oh, Beast!" she wept, "Oh, Beast! I did not mean to stay away so long. Please do not die. Please come back to me. You are so good and kind." She knelt and kissed his ugly head.

Suddenly no Beast was there, but a handsome prince stood before her. "Beauty, my dear one," he said, "I was bewitched by a spell that could only be broken when a beautiful girl loved me and wanted me in spite of my ugliness. When you kissed me just now you broke the enchantment."

Beauty rode with the prince to her father's house and then they all went together to the prince's kingdom. There he and Beauty were married. In time they became king and queen, and ruled for many happy years.

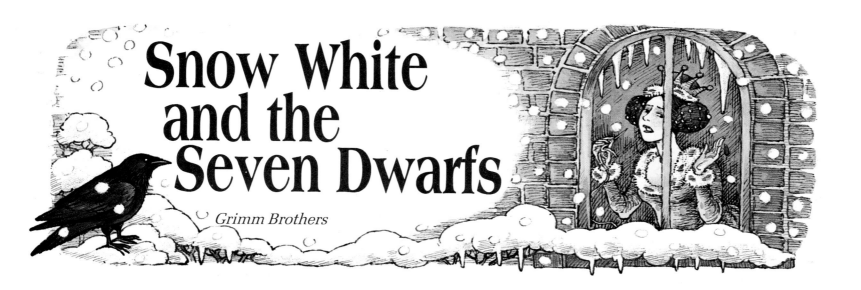

Snow White and the Seven Dwarfs

Grimm Brothers

One winter a beautiful queen sat sewing by a window. As she gazed down at the snow-covered garden she saw a black raven and her needle accidentally pricked her finger. A drop of blood fell on the snow. The colors were so strong that the queen said to herself, "If only I could have a child as white as snow, as black as a raven, and as red as blood."

Not long afterward the queen had a baby daughter, and when she saw her jet black hair, snowy white skin, and red red lips she remembered her strange wish on a winter's day and named her Snow White.

Snow White was a pretty little girl but after a few years, sad to say, her mother died and her father married again. The new queen, Snow White's stepmother, was very beautiful too, but she was very proud and vain. She had a magic mirror, and each day she would admire herself in it and ask:

"Mirror, mirror, on the wall,
Who is the fairest one of all?"
and the mirror would always reply:
"You, O Queen, are the fairest one of all."

The queen would smile when she heard this for she knew the mirror always spoke the truth. Years went by and Snow White grew prettier and prettier until one day when the queen looked in the magic mirror, the mirror replied:

"You, O Queen, are fair, 'tis true,
But Snow White is fairer now than you."

The queen was filled with envy. From that day she hated Snow White and her anger grew until finally she called for a hunter and told him to take Snow White deep into the forest and then to kill her.

"Cut out her heart and bring it back to prove she is really dead," she commanded.

The hunter felt very sad. Like everyone in the king's household he loved Snow White, but he knew he must obey the queen's orders. He took Snow White deep into the forest and pulled out his knife. Snow White fell to her knees. She looked so beautiful that the hunter took pity and told her to hide. Then he killed a deer and cut out its heart to take back to the cruel queen.

Snow White was frightened in the forest. She started to run here and there through the trees until in the evening she came to a clearing and found a little house. She wondered if it was a woodman's cottage where she might be able to stay, so she knocked at the door. There was no answer, so Snow White pushed it open and went inside.

There she saw a room all neat and tidy with a long table laid with seven places — seven knives and forks, seven wooden plates, and drinking cups. Snow White was so hungry and thirsty that she ate a little food from each plate and drank a little drop from each cup. She did not want to empty one person's plate and cup only.

Beyond the table were seven little beds all neatly made. Snow White tried them all out and the seventh bed was just right. She lay down and fell into a deep sleep for she was exhausted by her long journey through the forest.

The cottage was the home of seven dwarfs. All day long they worked in a mine nearby, digging diamonds from deep inside the mountain. When they returned home that night, they were startled to see that someone had entered their cottage and had taken some food and drink from each place at their table. They were more surprised to find their beds disturbed until the seventh dwarf found Snow White in his bed and called to the others. The seven dwarfs gathered around her. They marveled at her beauty but they decided not to disturb her for they were kind little men.

When Snow White awoke the next day she met the dwarfs and told them her story. "I have no home now," she said sadly, and at once the dwarfs asked her to stay with them in the cottage. Snow White agreed happily, and each morning when the dwarfs went off to work, she stayed behind and kept their cottage clean and cooked their supper.

The dwarfs warned Snow White that when she was alone she must beware of any strangers who might come to the cottage. They suspected that her stepmother had magic powers and would soon find out that Snow White had not been killed by the hunter.

Back at the palace the queen welcomed the hunter when he returned with the deer's heart. She was happy that once again she was the most beautiful woman in the world. As soon as she was alone she looked in her magic mirror and said:

"Mirror, mirror, on the wall,
Who is the fairest one of all?"

To her horror, the mirror replied:

"You, O Queen, are fair, 'tis true,
But Snow White is fairer still than you."

The queen shook with anger as she realized that the old hunter had tricked her. She decided that she would seek out Snow White and kill her herself.

The queen disguised herself as an old pedlar woman with a tray of ribbons and pretty things to sell and she set off into the forest. When she came to the dwarfs' cottage she knocked and cried out: "Pretty goods for sale! Pretty goods for sale!"

Snow White came to the door and looked eagerly at the tray. The queen noticed that she was attracted by some lacing ribbons and so she asked if Snow White would like to try one on. Then she tugged the lacing so tight that Snow White could not breathe and fell to the ground as if she were dead. The queen hurried to her palace, sure that this time Snow White was truly dead.

When the dwarfs returned that evening, they found Snow White lying on the floor, deathly cold and still. They rushed toward her in horror but soon noticed that she had a new lacing on her dress which had been tied too tightly. Quickly they cut it and Snow White started breathing again.

All seven dwarfs gave a tremendous sigh of relief as by now they loved Snow White dearly. She told them what had happened and the dwarfs begged her not to allow strangers into the cottage while she was alone.

Meanwhile back at the palace the queen asked the mirror:

"Mirror, mirror, on the wall,
Who is the fairest one of all?"

and the mirror replied:

"You, O Queen, are fair, 'tis true,
But Snow White is fairer still than you."

The queen was speechless with rage. She realized that yet again her plan to kill Snow White had failed. She resolved to try again and this time she was determined to succeed. She chose an apple with one rosy red side and one yellow side. Carefully she injected poison into the red part of the apple and placed it in a basket of apples.

The wicked queen, disguised this time as a peasant woman, then set out once more into the forest. Once more she knocked at the door of the dwarfs' cottage and waited for Snow White. The queen guessed that Snow White would have been warned not to buy anything from strangers so she quickly declared that she had nothing to sell. She simply chatted to Snow White and, as Snow White became less scared, she offered her an apple as a present. Snow White was tempted as the rosy apple looked delicious, but she refused, explaining that she had been told to accept nothing from strangers.

"I will show you how harmless it is," said the disguised queen. "First I will bite it and if I am unharmed, you will know it is safe for you too."

The queen had not poisoned the yellow side so she took a bite from there. When nothing happened, Snow White stretched out her hand for the apple. She also took a bite, but from the rosy red side. Instantly the poison attacked Snow White and she fell down as though dead.

That evening when the dwarfs returned they could not manage to revive her. They looked closely to make sure her dress was not laced too tightly. But they could find nothing different about her. All that night they watched over her, but when morning came, she did not move or breathe or speak, and they decided she must be dead. Weeping bitterly, they laid her in a coffin and placed a glass lid over the top so that all could admire her beauty, even though she was dead. Then they carried the coffin to the top of a hill where day and night they stood guard over their beautiful Snow White.

The wicked queen was delighted that day when she looked in her mirror and asked:

"Mirror, mirror, on the wall,
Who is the fairest one of all?"

and the mirror replied:

"You, O Queen, are the fairest one of all."

She gave a cruel laugh when she heard those words.

Then it happened that a prince came riding through the forest and saw the coffin on the hill. Snow White looked so beautiful that he fell in love at once and he begged the dwarfs to allow him to take the coffin with him to his own country. The dwarfs loved Snow White too much to permit him to do this, but they agreed to let the prince kiss her.

As the prince gently kissed Snow White, he moved her head. The piece of poisoned apple fell from her lips. She stirred, yawned and stretched a little. Moments later she was alive again.

"Where am I?" she asked, looking at the prince.

"Safe with me," replied the prince, and Snow White, too, fell in love.

Far away in her palace the wicked queen gazed in her mirror and the mirror said:

"You, O Queen, are fair 'tis true,
But Snow White is fairer still than you."

The queen cursed Snow White in fury. How had she escaped death once more? By now, the king had discovered what evil deeds the queen had planned and banished her from his kingdom. That night she left the palace and no one ever saw her or her mirror again.

Snow White said farewell to her kind friends, the dwarfs, and rode away with the prince. They were married at his father's castle and lived for a long time afterward in happiness and peace.

Brer Rabbit's New House

Joel Chandler Harris

Long ago an old man called Uncle Remus used to tell stories to a little boy. The two of them lived on a plantation in the south, and the stories were always about certain animals, Brer Rabbit and Brer Fox in particular, but several others too, Brer Bear and Brer Possum for instance. All too often Brer Rabbit, who was an impudent scoundrel, came out best, although he was one of the smaller creatures. Of course, to do this he had to use his wits.

One evening, Uncle Remus ate his supper as usual and then looked over his spectacles at the child.

"Now then, honey," he said. "Let's see if I can call to mind how old Brer Rabbit got himself a two-story house without paying much for it."

He paused a moment. Then he began:

It turned out one time that a whole lot of creatures decided to build a house together. Old Brer Bear, he was among them, and Brer Fox and Brer Wolf and Brer Coon and Brer Possum, and possibly Brer Mink too. Anyway, there was a whole bunch of them, and they set to work and built a house in less than no time.

Brer Rabbit, he pretended it made his head swim to climb the scaffolding, and that it made him feel dizzy to work in the sun, but he got a board, and he stuck a pencil behind his ear, and he went around measuring and marking, measuring and marking.

He looked so busy that all the other creatures were sure he was doing the most work, and folks going along the road said, "My, my, that Brer Rabbit is doing more work than the whole lot of them put together." Yet all the time Brer Rabbit was doing nothing, and he had plenty of time to lie in the shade.

Meanwhile, the other creatures, they built the house, and it sure was a fine one. It had an upstairs and a downstairs, and chimneys all around, and it had rooms for all the creatures who had helped to make it.

Brer Rabbit, he picked out one of the upstairs rooms, and he got a gun and a brass cannon, and when no one was looking he put them up in the room. Then he got a big bowl of dirty water and carried it up there when no one was looking.

When the house was finished and all the animals were sitting in the parlor after supper, Brer Rabbit, he got up and stretched himself, and made excuses, saying he believed he'd go to his room. When he got there, and while all the others were laughing and chatting and being sociable downstairs, Brer Rabbit stuck his head out of the room and hollered.

"When a big man wants to sit down, whereabouts is he going to sit?" says he.

The other creatures laughed, and called back, "If a big man like you can't sit in a chair he'd better sit on the floor."

"Watch out, down there," says old Brer Rabbit, "because I'm going to sit down," says he.

With that, *bang!* went Brer Rabbit's gun. The other creatures looked around at one another in astonishment as much as to say, "What in the name of gracious is that?"

They listened and listened, but they didn't hear any more fuss and it wasn't long before they were all chatting and talking again.

Then Brer Rabbit stuck his head out of his room again, and hollered, "When a big man like me wants to sneeze, whereabouts is he going to sneeze?"

The other creatures called back, "A big man like you can sneeze anywhere he wants."

"Watch out down there, then," says Brer Rabbit, "because I'm going to sneeze right here," says he.

With that Brer Rabbit let off his cannon – *bulder-um-m-m!* The window panes rattled. The whole house shook as though it would come down, and old Brer Bear fell out of his rocking chair – *kerblump!*

When they all settled down again Brer Possum and Brer Mink suggested that as Brer Rabbit had such a bad cold they would step outside and get some fresh air. The other creatures said that they would stick it out, and before long they all got their hair smoothed down and began to talk again.

After a while, when they were beginning to enjoy themselves once more, Brer Rabbit hollered out:

"When a big man like me chews tobacco, where is he going to spit?"

The other creatures called back as though they were getting pretty angry:

"Big man or little man, spit where you please!"

Then Brer Rabbit called out, "This is the way a big man spits," and with that he tipped over the bowl of dirty water, and when the other creatures heard it coming sloshing down the stairs, my, how they rushed out of the house! Some went out the back door, some went out the front door, some fell out of the windows, some went one way and some another way; but they all got out as quickly as they could.

Then Brer Rabbit, he shut up the house, and fastened the windows and went to bed. He pulled the covers up around his ears, and he slept like a man who doesn't owe anybody anything.

"And neither did he owe them," said Uncle Remus to the little boy, "for if the other creatures got scared and ran off from their own house, what business is that of Brer Rabbit? That's what I'd like to know."

Country Mouse, City Mouse

Aesop's Fables

There was once a little mouse who lived very happily in the country. He ate grains of wheat and grass seeds, nibbled turnips in the fields, and had a safe snug house in a hedgerow. On sunny days he would curl up on the bank near his nest and warm himself, and in the winter he would scamper in the fields with his friends.

He was delighted when he heard his cousin from the city was coming to visit him, and fetched some of the best food from his store cupboard so he could share it with him. When his cousin arrived, he proudly offered him some fine grains of dried wheat and some particularly good nuts he had put away in the autumn.

His cousin, the city mouse, however, was not impressed. "You call this good food?" he asked. "My dear fellow, you must come and stay with me in the city. I will then show you what fine living is all about. Come with me tomorrow, for not a day should be lost before you see the excellent hospitality I can offer."

So the two mice traveled up to the city. From his cousin's mousehole, the country mouse watched with wonder a grand dinner which the people who lived in the house were giving. He stared in amazement at the variety of cheese, the beautiful vegetables, the fresh white rolls, the fruit, and the wine served from glittering decanters.

"Now's our chance," said the city mouse, as the dining room emptied. The two mice came out of the hole, and scurried across the floor to where the crumbs lay scattered beneath the table. Never had the country mouse eaten such delicacies, or tasted such fine food. "My cousin was right," he thought as he nibbled at a fine juicy grape. "This is the good life!"

All of a sudden a great fierce furry beast leaped into the room and pounced on the mice.

"Run for it, little cousin!" shouted the city mouse, and together they reached the mousehole gasping for breath and shaking with fright. The cat settled down outside the hole, tail twitching, to wait for them.

"Don't worry. He will get bored soon, and go and amuse himself elsewhere. We can then go and finish our feast," said the city mouse.

"You can go out there again, if you like," said the country mouse. "I shall not. I am leaving tonight by the back door to return to my country home. I would rather gnaw a humble vegetable there than live here amid these dangers."

So the country mouse lived happily in the country, the city mouse in the city. Each was content with the way of life he was used to, and had no desire to change.

Sleeping Beauty

Charles Perrault

Long ago there lived a king and queen who had no children, which made them very sad. Then, one day, the queen was delighted to find she was going to have a baby. She and the king looked forward with great excitement to the day of their baby's birth.

When that day came, a lovely daughter was born and they arranged a large party for her Christening. They invited many guests including twelve fairies as they felt certain the fairies would make wishes for the new princess, their little daughter.

At the Christening party, the guests and the fairies all agreed that the princess was a beautiful baby. One fairy wished for her the gift of Happiness, another Beauty, others Wisdom, Health, Goodness, Contentment... Eleven fairies had made their wishes when suddenly the gates of the castle flew open and in swept a thirteenth fairy. She was furious that she had not been invited to the Christening party, and as she glared around a shiver ran down everyone's spine. Everyone felt her evil spirit. She waved her wand over the baby and cast not a wish but a terrible spell.

"On her sixteenth birthday," she hissed, "the princess will prick herself with a spindle. And she will die." A terrible hush fell over the queen and king and their guests.

The twelfth fairy had not yet made her wish and now she hesitated. She had been going to give the gift of Joy to the baby but now she wanted to stop the princess dying when she became sixteen. Her magic was not strong enough to break the wicked spell, but she could weaken its evil. So she wished that the princess would fall asleep for a hundred years instead of dying.

As she grew up the princess became the happiest, sweetest, and most beautiful child anyone had ever seen. It seemed as though all the wishes of the first eleven fairies had come true. The king and queen hoped to prevent the wicked fairy's spell from working by making sure that the princess never saw a spindle. All spinning was forbidden everywhere and all the cotton and wool in their country had to be sent away to be spun.

For their daughter's sixteenth birthday the king and queen decided to give a party in the castle. They felt sure there would be no chance of her finding a spindle there on that day.

People came from far and near to the grand birthday ball for the princess and a magnificent feast was provided. After all the guests had eaten and drunk as much as they wanted and danced in the great hall, the princess asked if they could all play hide-and-seek. She ran off to a far corner of the castle and found herself climbing a spiral staircase in a turret she did not remember even noticing before. "They will never find me here," she thought as she crept into a little room at the top. To her astonishment there was an old woman dressed in black sitting on a stool spinning.

"What are you doing?" questioned the princess as she saw the twirling spindle. She was puzzled as she had never seen anything like it anywhere in the kingdom.

"Come closer, pretty girl," replied the old woman. She pulled strands of wool from the sheep's fleece on the floor, then twisting it neatly with her fingers she fed it through the spindle. The princess was fascinated and edged nearer.

"Would you like to try?" the spinner asked cunningly.

The princess forgot all about playing hide-and-seek and she picked up the spindle. In a flash she pricked her thumb and as she cried for help, she fell down as though dead. The wicked fairy's spell had come true in the end.

But so did the twelfth good fairy's wish. The princess did not die but fell into a deep deep sleep. The spell worked upon everyone in the castle that evening. The king and queen slept on their thrones in the great hall. The guests dropped off to sleep even as they played hide-and-seek with the princess, while in the kitchen the cook fell asleep with her hand raised to box the pot boy's ears. All over the castle a great silence descended.

As time went by a thick thorn hedge grew up around the castle. Passers-by wondered what lay behind the hedge but no one now remembered the castle where the king and queen had lived with their lovely daughter. Sometimes curious travelers tried to force their way through but the hedge was so prickly that they soon gave up.

One day, many many years later, a prince came traveling by. Like the others, he was eager to know what was hidden behind the tall, thick thorn hedge. An old man told him a story he had heard long ago about a mysterious castle there and the prince became curious. He decided to cut his way through the thorns. In no time the hedge seemed to open out before his sword and very soon the young prince was inside the grounds. He ran across the gardens and through an open door into the lovely old castle.

Everywhere he looked — in the great hall, in the kitchens, in the ballroom and on the staircase — he saw people asleep. He hurried through many rooms until he found himself climbing a winding stair to an old turret. There in the small room at the top he was startled to see on the floor the most beautiful girl he had ever seen. She was so lovely that without thinking he knelt down and kissed her gently.

The spell was broken! The princess opened her eyes and fell in love with the prince immediately. She told him what had happened and he kissed her gently again. Together they came down the turret stairs and saw that the castle was coming alive.

In the great hall the king and queen were stretching and yawning, puzzled and worried that they had dropped off to sleep during their daughter's party. Their guests too were shaking their heads, rubbing their eyes, and wondering why they felt so sleepy. In the kitchen the cook boxed the ears of the pot boy. Outside horses neighed, dogs barked, and birds burst into song. The hundred year spell had been completely broken.

The princess told her parents that she truly loved the handsome young man who had kissed her and they were delighted to discover he was a prince from a nearby country. The king gave the couple his blessing and a grand wedding was arranged.

At the wedding the princess looked more beautiful than ever, and the prince fell in love with her all over again. The twelve good fairies who had come to her Christening were invited once more and everyone rejoiced to see the happiness of the prince and the princess. Toward evening they rode off together to their new home in the prince's kingdom where they lived happily ever afterward.

The Little House

Traditional Russian

Once upon a time a large earthenware jar rolled off the back of a cart that was going to market. It came to rest in the grass at the side of the road.

By and by a mouse came along and looked at the jar. "What a fine house that would make," he thought, and he called out:

"Little house, little house,
Who lives in the little house?"

Nobody answered, so the mouse peeped in and saw that it was empty. He moved in right away and began to live there.

Before long a frog came along and saw the jar. "What a fine house that would make," he thought, and he called out:

"Little house, little house,
Who lives in the little house?"
and he heard:

"I, Mr. Mouse.
I live in the little house.
Who are you?"

"I am Mr. Frog," came the reply.

"Come in Mr. Frog, and we can live here together," called out the mouse.

So the mouse and the frog lived happily together in the little house. Then one day a hare came running along the road and saw the little house. He called out:

"Little house, little house,
Who lives in the little house?"

and he heard:

"Mr. Frog and Mr. Mouse,
We live in the little house.
Who are you?"

"I am Mr. Hare," he replied.

"Come in, Mr. Hare, and live with us," called the mouse and the frog.

The hare went in and settled down with the frog and the mouse in the little house.

Some time later a fox came along, and spied the little house. "That would make a fine house," he thought, and he called out:

"Little house, little house,
Who lives in the little house?"

and he heard:

"Mr. Hare, Mr. Frog and Mr. Mouse,
We all live in the little house.
Who are you?"

"I am Mr. Fox," he replied.

"Then come in and live with us, Mr. Fox," they called back.

Mr. Fox went in and found there was just room for him too, although it was a bit of a squeeze.

The next day a bear came ambling along the road, and saw the little house. He called out:

"Little house, little house,
Who lives in the little house?"

and he heard:

"Mr. Fox, Mr. Hare, Mr. Frog, and Mr. Mouse,
We all live in the little house.
Who are you?"

"I am Mr. Bear Squash-you-all-flat," said the bear.

He then sat down on the little house, and squashed it all flat.
That was the end of the little house.

The Black Bull of Norroway

Traditional Scottish and Scandinavian

Long ago, in a country far away in the north there lived a widow and her three daughters. She had once been a queen, but her husband, the king, had been killed in a battle and she was now very, very poor.

One day her eldest daughter said to her, "Mother, bake me a cake to take to the fortune-teller so that she will tell me my fortune."

The fortune-teller accepted the fine cake the girl had brought, and then she said to her, "Stand by the back door, my dear, and tell me if anything comes down the road."

By and by the girl cried out that a carriage drawn by six gray horses was coming toward them.

"Go with it," said the fortune-teller, "for there your fortune lies."

Before long the second daughter asked her mother to bake a cake for the fortune-teller, for she too wanted to know what life had to offer her.

"Stand by the back door, my dear," said the fortune-teller, "and tell me if anything comes down the road." When a carriage drawn by six gleaming chestnut horses came by, she told the girl to get into it, for there lay her fortune.

In time the youngest asked her mother to bake a cake for her to take to the fortune-teller. Just as before, the fortune-teller said, "Stand by the back door, my dear, and tell me if anything comes down the road." Soon the girl saw a great black bull.

"Go with the bull, girl," said the fortune-teller, "for your fortune lies with the bull."

The young girl was very disappointed, for she wanted to drive away in a fine carriage like her sisters, but she did as the fortune-teller told her.

She rode on the back of the great black bull for many miles, until she was faint with hunger and thirst. "Eat out of my left ear," said the bull, "and drink out of my right." The girl did as he suggested and to her amazement found in each ear all the food and drink she wanted.

In the evening they came to a fine castle. "We will spend the night here," said the bull, "in my brother's castle."

The girl was lifted off his back and taken into the castle while the bull was led into a field. To her surprise she found her eldest sister living there as the lady of the house. They greeted each other joyfully, then her sister said, "The black bull is really the Lord of Norroway. A spell was cast many years ago which turned him into a bull."

That night the girl slept in great luxury and the next day her sister gave her a beautiful apple. "Keep it," she said, and do not break it, until you are in great trouble."

All that day the girl traveled on the black bull's back, until evening when they came to another fine castle. "We will stay the night here, in this castle where my second brother lives," said the bull.

This time the girl found her other sister living there as a grand lady. She spent the night in a room hung with gold tapestries and in the morning her sister gave her a pear.

"Keep it safe," she said, "until the day when you are in great need. Only then should you break it open."

That day, the girl and the black bull traveled on again. Further and further they journeyed – further than the girl thought possible. She was exhausted when they arrived in the evening at a castle that was grander than any of the others she had seen.

"This is my home," said the bull, "and we will stay here for tonight." The girl was well looked after as before and the next morning she was given a beautiful plum.

"Keep this carefully," she was told, "until the day when you are in great need. Only then should you break it open."

On the fourth day the great black bull took her to a deep dark valley, where he asked her to get off his back. "You must stay here," he said, "while I go and fight the devil. You will know if I win, for everything around will turn blue, but if I lose, everything you see will turn red. Sit on this boulder and remember you must not move, not even a hand or a foot, until I return. For if you move, I shall never find you again."

The girl promised to do as she was told, for by now she loved and trusted the bull. For hours and hours she sat on the boulder without moving, then, just when she felt she could wait no longer, everything around her suddenly went blue. She was so delighted that she moved one foot. She moved it only a little, just enough to cross it over the other, forgetting her promise for a moment.

The bull returned after his victory but, just as he had said, he could not find her anywhere. The girl stayed in the valley for hours, weeping for what she had done, and at last she set off alone, although she did not know where to go.

After she had wandered from valley to valley for several days, the young girl came to a glass mountain. She tried to climb it, but each time her feet slipped backward, and eventually she gave up. Soon after this she met a blacksmith who told her that if she worked for him for seven years he would make her special shoes of iron that would take her over the glass mountain.

For seven long years she worked hard for the blacksmith, and at the end of that time he kept his promise and made her the shoes to take her on her way. On the other side of the mountain she stopped at a little house where a washerwoman and her daughter were scrubbing some bloodstained clothes in a tub.

"The finest lord I have ever seen left these clothes here seven years ago," said the washerwoman. "He told us that whoever washed out the bloodstains would be his wife. But for seven long years we have washed and rinsed, and the stains remain."

"Let me try," said the girl, and the first time she washed the clothes the bloodstains disappeared. Absolutely delighted, the washerwoman rushed off and told the lord of the castle nearby that the clothes were clean. Now this lord was the Lord of Norroway, and the old woman lied to him, saying that it was her own daughter who had done the task. She thought it would be a fine thing for her daughter to marry a lord. The wedding was arranged for the next day, and there seemed nothing the young girl could do to stop it.

Then she remembered the apple she had been given so long ago. Surely the time had come to open it. Inside were jewels, which sparkled and shone. She showed these to the washerwoman, and asked if she could see the lord alone that evening. "The jewels will all be yours if you arrange this for me," she said.

The washerwoman took the jewels greedily, but before she allowed the girl to go to the lord's room, she put a sleeping potion in his drink, so that he slept deeply the whole night through.

The girl sat by his bedside, and she cried:
"Seven long years I served for thee,
The glassy hill I climbed for thee,
The bloodstained clothes I washed for thee,
Wilt thou not wake, and turn to me?"
but the Lord of Norroway slept on.

The next day the girl was overcome with grief because she had failed to stop the wedding, so she broke open the pear. It contained even more lovely jewels than the apple. She took these to the washerwoman. "Marry your daughter tomorrow," she begged once again, "not today, and let me see the lord alone once more. In return the jewels will be yours."

The washerwoman agreed, but again slipped a sleeping potion into the lord's drink.

For the second time the girl sat by his bedside and cried:
"Seven long years I served for thee,
The glassy hill I climbed for thee,
The bloodstained clothes I washed for thee,
Wilt thou not wake and turn to me?"
but the Lord of Norroway slept on.

The next morning the girl broke open the beautiful plum she had been given, and found an even greater collection of splendid jewels. She offered them to the greedy washerwoman who agreed to put off the wedding one more day. That night she once more put the sleeping potion into the lord's drink. But this time the lord poured away the drink when the washerwoman was not looking for he suspected trickery of some kind.

When the girl came to his room for the third time and cried:

"Seven long years I served for thee,
The glassy hill I climbed for thee,
The bloodstained clothes I washed for thee,
Wilt thou not wake and turn to me?"

the Lord of Norroway turned and saw her.

As they talked he told her his story: how a spell had been cast on him turning him into a bull, how he had fought and beaten the devil and the spell had been broken. "Ever since then," he said, "I have been searching for you."

The Lord of Norroway and the youngest daughter were married next day, and lived happily in the castle. "I little thought," she said, "the day I saw the black bull coming down the road, that I had truly found my fortune."

The Rats' Daughter

Traditional Eastern

Mr. and Mrs. Rat had the most beautiful daughter. She had the longest, slinkiest tail you could imagine, and the most remarkable long elegant whiskers. Her silky coat was a lovely glowing pinkish brown color, and her teeth were gleaming white with sharp points. She was in every way a very lovely young rat.

Mr. Rat was hoping to find a handsome young rat as a husband for this daughter. Mrs. Rat, however, was more ambitious and hoped to marry her daughter to the most powerful creature in the world.

"I have been thinking, my dear," she said to Mr. Rat one day, "that there is nothing more powerful in the world than the Sun. I feel sure the Sun would like to marry our lovely daughter."

Mr. Rat was rather taken aback by this idea, but seeing that his wife's mind was made up, he agreed. So they all set off to call on the Sun.

Now the Sun was not at all interested in the idea of marrying a rat – even a very beautiful rat – but he listened politely to what the parents had to say, and thought for a few moments before replying.

"You flatter me when you say I am the most powerful thing in the world, for I am not as powerful as that Cloud you can see over there. He can stand in front of me, and shut off my light and heat whenever he wants. I think your daughter would do better to marry the Cloud."

Mr. and Mrs. Rat were delighted with his suggestion, for they could see at once that what the Sun had said was true. Certainly the Cloud was more powerful than the Sun, for at any time he could cover the Sun whether the Sun wanted it or not. "We should go to the Cloud with our daughter," they agreed, "and offer him the chance to marry a bride of the greatest beauty."

The Cloud was rather surprised when Mr. and Mrs. Rat called on him to offer him their daughter's hand in marriage. He agreed with them that she was indeed a most beautiful rat, but he did not like the idea of marrying her at all. He considered carefully before replying.

"My friend the Sun is kind to describe me as the most powerful thing in the world but I'm afraid he's mistaken. The Wind is far more powerful than I am. The Wind can blow me across the sky at a moment's notice. I think you should call on the Wind and suggest he marries your daughter."

Mr. and Mrs. Rat saw at once that what the Cloud said was true so they took their daughter to visit the Wind.

The Wind stopped blowing for a few minutes to talk to the Rat family, but he did not like the idea of marrying at all. He was far too busy to stay still in one place for long, even for a few minutes.

So the Wind said to Mr. and Mrs. Rat:

"The Cloud was right to say I am more powerful than he, but have you considered that the Wall over there is more powerful than me? However hard I blow, I can never blow him down. I think you should take your beautiful daughter to him. He is the most powerful of all."

The Wind rushed off, leaving Mr. and Mrs. Rat nodding at his wisdom. "Come along child," they said to their daughter. "We will go and see the Wall. He will surely be glad to have such a beautiful bride."

When they arrived at the Wall, Mr. and Mrs. Rat bowed low before him, for they could see he was extremely strong and powerful. They explained that they had come to offer him their beautiful daughter as a wife and the Wall replied that he would think over the idea very carefully. But while he was thinking, there was a sudden and unexpected interruption.

"I don't want to marry a Wall," shouted Miss Rat, twitching her whiskers and stamping her foot. "I would have married the Sun, or the Cloud, or the Wind, but I don't want to have a Wall for my husband," and she burst into tears.

Mr. and Mrs. Rat were horrified at their daughter's rudeness, but the Wall said with great tact, "Your daughter is right. She should not marry me. There is only one animal who can reduce me, a Wall, into dust. That animal is the rat, who can gnaw through me with his sharp teeth. I would advise you to marry your daughter to the finest rat you can find. She will never have a more powerful husband."

And so it ended happily. Mr. Rat was glad because he had always thought there was no finer creature on earth than the rat. Mrs. Rat was pleased now that she knew how powerful a rat husband would be. As for the Rats' daughter, she thought she would be very happy indeed married to a handsome young rat.

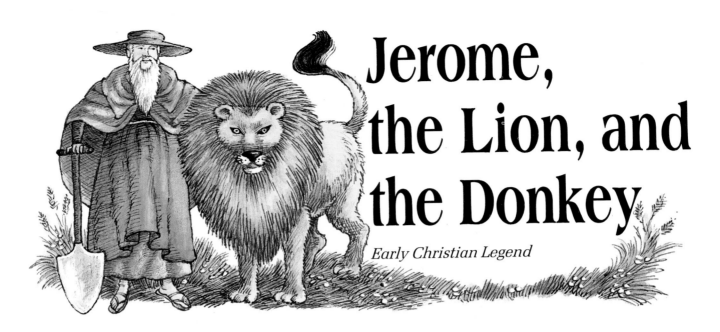

Jerome, the Lion, and the Donkey

Early Christian Legend

Jerome was a holy man who lived in a monastery many hundreds of years ago. One hot afternoon, he and some of the other monks were sitting together, when a lion appeared in the courtyard of the monastery. There was panic and confusion as several of the monks thought the lion had come to kill them, but then Jerome saw that the lion was limping.

"Calm yourselves, brothers," he said, "and bring me some clean cloths and warm water. The poor creature has come to us for help. We need not be afraid of him."

Cautiously they gathered around, and one man fetched warm water, another a clean cloth for a bandage, and another some ointment made from healing herbs. Very gently, Jerome bathed and bandaged the torn foot. The lion then lay down peacefully in the shade of the courtyard and slept.

The next day the lion was still there, and Jerome bathed his paw again. It was less swollen, and again the lion seemed grateful for the help he had received. So it was for several days, until the paw was completely healed. The monks were pleased to hear he was cured, as they thought he would now go away.

But the lion did not go. He stayed and followed Jerome when he went to work in the fields, and lay down in the courtyard when Jerome was in the monastery. Several monks felt certain that a fully grown lion, no longer in pain, must be savage, and that sooner or later someone would be hurt. But whenever they tried sending the lion away he always came back to the monastery.

"It's no good," said Jerome. "He has come to stay."

"It is not right that he should stay for he does no work," said one of the monks. "None of us stays here without working."

So Jerome said, "Well, let us think of some work he can do."

Then one old monk whose job it was to take the donkey to the woods every day to collect logs for the fire, said, "Let the lion go with the donkey each day. He will stop wild beasts attacking the donkey better than I can, and I will then be free to do other jobs."

So it was agreed, and each day the lion and the donkey set out together for the woods. On the way the donkey would eat grass in the pasture while the lion guarded him. The woodmen would then fill the baskets that were strapped to the donkey's back with logs, and together they would return.

"What a useful member of the community he is," said some of the monks, while others still took care not to get too close.

One day, as the donkey was grazing, the lion found a shady spot to lie and wait for his friend, and in the still of the hot day he dropped off to sleep. As he slept some traveling merchants with a string of camels came by, and saw the donkey grazing alone.

"Look at that," they said to each other. "A donkey is just what we want to lead our camels. No one seems to be looking after it. Let's take it quickly."

The merchants threw the donkey's baskets behind a bush, and led him off at the head of their camels.

When the lion awoke and found the donkey had disappeared, he roared in misery. That evening he returned to the monastery, his head hanging low with shame. The monks crowded around him, wondering where the donkey was.

"A wild beast should never be trusted," some of them said. "He has killed and eaten our dear donkey, even after all these months of appearing to be such a gentle animal."

Jerome said, "Do not judge him too quickly, brothers. Let us go to the wood and see if we find something to show us what happened to the donkey."

So a group of monks set off, and when they found the donkey's baskets, they said, "Look, here is the evidence we wanted. This shows the donkey was killed by the savage lion."

But the lion still showed no sign of being fierce, so Jerome suggested to the angry monks that the lion should now do the

donkey's work. "Let him go to the woods each day with the donkey's baskets strapped to his back," he said, "and let him carry the logs we need as the little donkey used to do."

The monks agreed to Jerome's plan, and each morning after that the lion set out for the woods alone to collect the logs.

A whole year went by, and during this time Jerome was made the head monk in the monastery. The lion, still Jerome's friend and companion, continued to go each day to get wood for the monastery. He did the task without complaining, almost as if he were saying, "I am sorry about the donkey," each time they strapped the baskets on him.

One day, when he was returning from the woods, the lion caught sight of his old friend the donkey. The traveling merchants were once more on their old route and the little donkey they had stolen was leading their string of camels. Without hesitating, the lion gave a great roar and bounded over to the donkey. The merchants, thinking they were being attacked by a wild and ferocious lion, fled in terror, while the donkey gave a bray of delight and trotted over to his friend the lion.

Together they set off toward the monastery, for the lion wished to show the monks that he had found the little donkey. For a whole year the camels had followed the donkey, and now they continued to do so. The merchants were all hiding and could do nothing to stop them.

At the monastery, the monks looked up in astonishment to see the strange procession of lion, donkey, and camels.

"I see," said Jerome, "that the lion has made good his fault. He has found the donkey he so carelessly lost a year ago. We have been harsh to think he might have killed him."

Just then the courtyard was filled with angry merchants who had followed the camels. Now they asked to speak to the head of the monastery, and Jerome stepped forward.

"You have stolen our donkey, our camels and all our wares," they shouted angrily. "We demand you return them at once."

"We have stolen nothing," Jerome replied quietly. "Your camels and the goods they carry are yours to take away. The camels came here of their own accord. But the donkey is not yours to take. He was ours, and he was stolen last year. It must have

been you who took him, and hid his baskets behind the bush. Now
he has come back with his friend the lion to his real owners.''

The merchants now looked ashamed. Promising they would
not steal again and still eyeing the lion with fear, they went on
their way, taking their camels and goods with them.

The donkey and the lion went out together each day as
before, and the monks who had thought the lion a savage beast
were sorry that they had misjudged him. The lion lived for many
more years in the monastery, and in his old age he would sit at
Jerome's feet as the holy man wrote books. The monastery was
known far and wide as a place where wisdom and gentleness were
always to be found.

The Princess and the Pea

Hans Christian Andersen

There was once a handsome prince who wanted to marry a princess. He traveled far and wide to find one and met a great many people, and quite a number of princesses, too. The trouble was that something was wrong with all the princesses, and after many months he returned home and told his parents, "I cannot find a princess to marry."

One night, not long after his return, a terrible storm broke over the palace. Lightning flashed, thunder crashed and the rain poured down. The prince and his parents heard someone knocking on the great front door. "Who would be out in such a storm?" they asked each other.

A girl stood shivering on the doorstep. Water streamed off her hair and down her face and her dress was soaked through. "Come in," cried the king. "Come in and tell us who you are."

"I am a p-p-p-princess," she replied through her chattering teeth. "I was looking for the king's palace, and I was caught in a storm." She did not look in the least like a princess, but the queen said to herself, "I believe I can find out if she is a princess or not."

While the girl was having a hot bath the queen went to prepare her bedroom. She sent two maids scurrying to collect mattresses and quilts from all over the palace. First she placed a dried pea underneath the bottom mattress and then more and more mattresses were piled onto the bed. In all twenty mattresses were placed on top of the pea. Then the queen told the maids to place twenty feather quilts on top of the mattresses. When the girl went to the bedroom she found her bed so high that she had to climb a ladder to get into it.

The next morning both the king and queen asked if she had slept well. "I am sorry to say, I had a very bad night," she told them. "There was a little hard lump in my bed and I tossed and turned all night. Now I am black and blue with bruises."

The queen was delighted. Only a real princess could have felt a pea through twenty mattresses and twenty quilts. She hurried off to tell the prince.

The prince married the princess and they lived happily for many years. As for the pea, it was put on display in a glass case in the town museum. When they saw it, people would say, "That really is some story, the story of the princess and the pea."

Pegasus the Winged Horse

Greek Legend

Long, long ago, there lived the fiercest monster imaginable, called the Chimera. He had three heads, each of them different, and could breathe fire from all three mouths at once. One head was shaped like a goat, one like a lion, and the third was in the form of a serpent. All might have been well if the monster had lived quietly in the mountains, but he was forever coming down into the cities and villages, eating people, destroying buildings and burning up crops on the farms. No one could get near enough to kill him and it looked as though the whole of the country would be destroyed by the Chimera.

The king of this land offered a great reward to anyone who would rid him of the Chimera. There was a young man called Bellerophon, who wanted to prove his bravery, and so he came forward. He had an idea that if he could attack the monster from the air he might have a chance of winning.

One night, in a dream, Athene, the Goddess of Wisdom, came to Bellerophon and told him about Pegasus, the winged horse of the gods, of the fountain where the horse liked to drink, and where he might find a golden bridle which would help him tame the horse. After a long journey Bellerophon reached the fountain and found the bridle of gold. He hid until Pegasus came to drink, then crept up and slipped the bridle over the horse's neck.

Pegasus, who had never been touched by a man before, jumped away, and as he did so Bellerophon leaped onto his back. A great struggle then took place between them for Pegasus tried every trick he knew to throw Bellerophon. He soared up into the sky; he twisted, bucked, reared, spun around. Somehow Bellerophon hung on, and at last he was able to get the bit into Pegasus's mouth. Soon after this Pegasus gave in and came to rest on the ground, his sides heaving with exhaustion.

Bellerophon explained to the beautiful white winged horse why he had captured him, and how he needed his help to save the kingdom from the fire-eating monster. As he spoke, he saw that there were tears in the horse's eyes, and said, "I cannot do this to you. It is no quarrel of yours. You shall go free and I must find some other way to win this victory." He took off the bridle and watched Pegasus soar into the sky.

In a few minutes, just as he was about to start his journey home, he felt a gentle nuzzle by his arm. To Bellerophon's delight the horse had returned of his own free will.

For many days they trained together so that they would have the best possible chance against the Chimera. At last, the day came. Bellerophon took out his finest armor, sharpened his sword and flew off on Pegasus's back to seek the monster.

The Chimera was outside his cave, preparing to raid another village. Before he knew what was happening, and without hearing more than a faint whirr in the air above him, he felt an agonizing blow. Bellerophon had chopped off one of his heads. It was the goat's head, and it lay in the dust while the monster roared with pain and lashed his tail with rage. Smoke and flames shot out in every direction as he tried to find his attacker.

Hidden by the smoke, Pegasus and Bellerophon were able to swoop down on him again and in a flash the sword swept through another neck. This time the lion's head rolled in the dust. The monster was wild and savage with pain and anger. He hurled himself at his attackers, and clung to Pegasus with his huge scaly claws as the horse rose into the air. Bellerophon thought they would surely die; the heat from the flames was terrible, and the serpent's head was only inches from his own. But the horse never wavered, soaring higher and higher into the air.

As the serpent's head stretched out to strike, Bellerophon saw a weak spot under its neck and drove his sword in with all his strength. The Chimera gave a ghastly scream. His hold on Pegasus loosened and he tumbled backward in a shower of sparks. He crashed to the ground burning as he went.

Bellerophon became a great hero, and so did the winged horse. They had other adventures together, but when Bellerophon tried to fly to heaven with Pegasus he was thrown. Some people said that Zeus, the king of the gods, was jealous, and sent an insect to tickle Pegasus and make him throw his rider. Pegasus went on flying up to heaven where he was changed into a group of stars, which you may see shining in the sky on a clear night.

The Fisherman's Son

Traditional Caucasian

Along time ago, when impossible things were possible, there was a fisherman and his son. One day when the fisherman hauled in his net he found huge gleaming red fish among the rest of his catch. For a few moments he was so excited he could only stare at it. "This fish will make me famous," he thought. "Never before has a fisherman caught such a fish."

"Stay here," he said to his son, "and look after these fish, while I go and fetch the cart to take them home."

The fisherman's son, too, was amazed by the great red fish, and while he was waiting for his father, he stroked it and started to talk to it.

"It seems a shame that a beautiful creature like you should not swim free," he said, and no sooner had he spoken than he decided to put the fish back into the sea. The great red fish slipped gratefully into the water, raised its head and spoke to the boy.

"It was kind of you to save my life. Take this bone which I have pulled from my fin. If ever you need my help, hold it up, call me, and I will come at once."

The fisherman's son placed the bone carefully in his pocket just as his father reappeared with the cart. When the father saw that the great red fish was gone he was angry beyond belief.

"Get out of my sight," he shouted at his son, "and never let me set eyes on you again."

The boy went off sadly. He did not know where to go or what to do. In time he found himself in a great forest. He walked on and on, till suddenly he was startled by a stag rushing through the trees toward him. It was being chased by a pack of ferocious hounds followed by hunters, and it was clearly exhausted and could run no further. The boy felt sorry for the stag and took hold of its antlers as the hounds and then the hunters appeared.

"Shame on you," he said, "for chasing a tame stag. Go and find a wild beast to hunt for your sport."

The hunters, seeing the stag standing quietly by the boy, thought it must be a pet and so they turned and rode off to another part of the forest.

"It was kind of you to save my life," said the stag, and it pulled a fine brown hair from its coat. "Take this and if ever you need help, hold it out and call me. I will come at once."

The fisherman's son put the hair in his pocket with the fishbone. He thanked the stag which disappeared among the trees and wandered on once more.

As he walked he heard a strange fluttering sound overhead and, looking up, he saw a great bird – a crane – being attacked by an eagle. The crane was weak and could fight no more, and the eagle was about to kill it. The kind-hearted boy picked up a stick and threw it at the eagle, which flew off at once, fearful of this new enemy. The crane sank to the ground.

"It was kind of you to save my life," it said as it recovered its breath. "Take this feather and keep it safe. If ever you need help, hold it out and call me, and I will come."

As the fisherman's son walked on with the feather in his pocket, he met a fox running for its life, with the hounds and the huntsmen close behind. The boy just had time to hide the fox under his coat before the hounds were all around him.

"I think the fox went that way," he cried to the huntsmen, and they called off the hounds and went in the direction the boy was pointing.

"It was kind of you to save my life," said the fox. "Take this hair from my coat and keep it safe. If ever you need help, hold it out and call me. I will come at once."

The fisherman's son went on his way, and in time he reached the edge of the forest and found himself by a lovely castle.

"Who lives there?" he asked.

"A beautiful princess," he was told. "Are you one of her suitors? She plays a curious game of hide-and-seek with all who come, and says she will marry the first man who hides so well that she cannot find him."

The fisherman's son thought he would try, so boldly he went to the castle and asked to see the princess. She was indeed very beautiful, and he thought what a fine thing it would be if he could marry her.

"Princess, I will hide where you cannot find me," he said, "but will you give me four chances?"

The princess was intrigued by this shabby boy, and agreed, thinking she would at least have some fun looking for him.

The fisherman's son went straightaway to the place where he had last seen the fish and, taking the fishbone from his pocket, he called its name.

"I am here," said the great red fish. "What can I do for you?"

"Can you take me where the princess will never find me? If you do, I shall be able to marry her."

The red fish took the boy on its back and swam deep down into the sea to some caverns where it hid him.

Now the princess had a magic mirror which she used in her games of hide-and-seek. With it she could see far and wide even through houses and hillsides. She looked in her mirror, but could not find the fisherman's son.

"What a wizard he must be," she said to herself, as she turned her mirror this way and that. Then she saw him sitting in a rocky cavern deep down in the sea and she laughed.

The next day when the boy came to the palace she smiled and said, "That was easy. You were deep down in a cavern under the sea. You will have to do better than that if you are going to marry me!"

"What an enchantress she must be," said the boy to himself, and he resolved to win this contest.

He went next to the forest and held out the stag's hair and called. When the stag came he told it that he wanted to hide and the stag took him on its back far far away to the other side of the mountains and hid him in a little cave. The stag then stood in front of the cave so that no one could see inside.

Once more the princess took out her mirror and searched far and wide for the boy. "How clever he is," she said to herself, and then the mirror picked him out hiding in the cave.

The next day she said to the boy, "Pooh! It was easy to see you in that cave."

The boy became even more determined to marry her and he set out to summon the crane. It came as soon as the boy waved the feather and called its name.

"Come with me high up into the clouds," said the crane, and took the boy on its back. All day long they hovered in the sky, while the princess searched this way and that in her mirror.

Just as she was about to give up, she spied him above her. "He is cleverer than I thought!" she said to herself.

But the next day when the boy came to the castle, she laughed and said, "You thought I would never find you among the clouds, but I spotted you easily. You only have one more chance to outwit me!"

The boy now went to the forest and, holding up the fox's hair he called the fox. When it came he explained what he wanted. "Ask her to give you fourteen days," said the fox, "and I should be able to hide you where she cannot find you."

The princess agreed, and for fourteen days the fox tunneled and dug beneath the princess's castle until it had made a hole large enough for the boy to hide in right under the princess's room. Down he went and lay there quietly. The princess took out her mirror and searched. She looked to the north, to the south, to the east, to the west; she looked high and low, round and round, and at last, exasperated, she called out:

"I give up. Where are you, fisherman's son?"

"Here!" he called. "Just below you!" And he jumped out from the hole the fox had dug.

"You win, wizard," she said, and was happy to marry the fisherman's son.

He was delighted to marry such a beautiful princess. They had a great wedding in the castle, and the celebrations went on for many days.

The Old Woman and her Pig

Traditional English

There was once an old woman who found some money under the floorboards of her house. "How lucky I am," she said. "I can go to the market and buy myself a pig."

So the old woman went to the market and bought herself a fine pig. Now it's easy to take a pig home from market if you have a truck or a cart, but the old woman had neither of these, so she had to walk home with the pig.

On the way she decided to take a short cut through the fields. But she had forgotten that there was a stile between two fields on her way and now, however hard she tried, the old woman could not make the pig climb over the stile.

The old woman saw a dog so she said:

"Dog! Dog! Bite the pig!

The pig won't climb over the stile,

and I shan't get home tonight!"

But the dog would not bite the pig.

Then the old woman saw a stick, and she said:

"Stick! Stick! Beat the dog!

The dog won't bite the pig,

The pig won't climb over the stile,

and I shan't get home tonight!"

But the stick would not beat the dog.

The old woman went a little farther and she found a fire, and she said:

"Fire! Fire! Burn the stick!

The stick won't beat the dog,

The dog won't bite the pig,

The pig won't climb over the stile,

and I shan't get home tonight!"

But the fire would not burn the stick.

The old woman was getting very cross wondering how she was ever going to get the pig over the stile, when she saw a bucket of water. So she said:

"Water! Water! Put out the fire!
The fire won't burn the stick,
The stick won't beat the dog,
The dog won't bite the pig,
The pig won't climb over the stile,
and I shan't get home tonight!"

But the water would not put out the fire.

The old woman went a little farther and she saw a bull standing in the field. So she said:

"Bull! Bull! Drink the water!
The water won't put out the fire,
The fire won't burn the stick,
The stick won't beat the dog,
The dog won't bite the pig,
The pig won't climb over the stile,
and I shan't get home tonight!"

But the bull would not drink the water.

The old woman went a little farther and met a butcher. So she said:

"Butcher! Butcher! Kill the bull!
The bull won't drink the water,
The water won't put out the fire,
The fire won't burn the stick,
The stick won't beat the dog,
The dog won't bite the pig,
The pig won't climb over the stile,
and I shan't get home tonight!"

But the butcher would not kill the bull.

The old woman went a little farther and saw a rope, and she said:

"Rope! Rope! Hang the butcher!
The butcher won't kill the bull,
The bull won't drink the water,
The water won't put out the fire,
The fire won't burn the stick,
The stick won't beat the dog,
The dog won't bite the pig,
The pig won't climb over the stile,
and I shan't get home tonight!"

But the rope would not hang the butcher.

Then the old woman went a little farther and caught sight of a rat, and she said:

"Rat! Rat! Gnaw the rope!
The rope won't hang the butcher,
The butcher won't kill the bull,
The bull won't drink the water,
The water won't put out the fire,
The fire won't burn the stick,
The stick won't beat the dog,
The dog won't bite the pig,
The pig won't climb over the stile,
and I shan't get home tonight!"

But the rat would not gnaw the rope.

The old woman wondered what on earth she was going to do when she saw a cat, and she said:

"Cat! Cat! Catch the rat!
The rat won't gnaw the rope,
The rope won't hang the butcher,
The butcher won't kill the bull,
The bull won't drink the water,
The water won't put out the fire,
The fire won't burn the stick,
The stick won't beat the dog,
The dog won't bite the pig,
The pig won't climb over the stile,
and I shan't get home tonight!"

The cat said, "If you bring me a saucer of milk I will catch the rat for you."

The old woman jumped for joy and ran over to a cow in the next field, crying, "Cow! Cow! Will you give me some milk for the cat?" and the cow said:

"If you bring me some hay from that haystack over there I will give you some milk."

So the old woman fetched some hay for the cow and the cow let the old woman milk her. She took the milk to the cat and the cat lapped it up.

Then the cat began to chase the rat,
The rat began to gnaw the rope,
The rope began to hang the butcher,
The butcher began to kill the bull,
The bull began to drink the water,
The water began to put out the fire,
The fire began to burn the stick,
The stick began to beat the dog,
The dog began to bite the pig,
The pig got a tremendous fright and leapt over the stile and the old lady got home that night.

Aladdin and his Wonderful Lamp

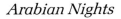

Arabian Nights

Far off in a beautiful city in China a ragged urchin called Aladdin used to play in the street. His father, a poor tailor, tried to make him work, but Aladdin was lazy and disobedient, and refused even to help in his father's shop. Even after his father died Aladdin still preferred to roam in the streets with his friends, and did not feel ashamed to eat the food his mother bought with the money she earned by spinning cotton.

One day a wealthy stranger came to the city. He noticed Aladdin in the street and thought, "That lad looks as though he has no purpose in life. It will not matter if I use him, then kill him."

The stranger quickly found out that Aladdin's father, Mustapha, was now dead. He called Aladdin over to him.

"Greetings, nephew," he said, "I am your father's brother. I have returned to China only to find my dear brother, Mustapha, is dead. Take this money and tell your mother I shall visit her."

Aladdin's mother was puzzled when Aladdin told her the stranger's message. "You have no uncle," she said. "I don't understand why this man should give us money."

The next day the stranger came to their house and talked about how he had loved his brother and offered to buy a fine shop where Aladdin could sell beautiful things to the rich people in the city. He gave Aladdin some new clothes and in a short while Aladdin's mother began to believe this man was a relation.

The stranger now invited Aladdin to go with him to the rich part of the city. Together they walked through beautiful gardens

and parks where Aladdin had never been before, until he found himself far from home. At last the stranger showed Aladdin a flat stone with an iron ring set into it.

"Lift this stone for me, nephew," he said, "and go into the cavern below. Walk through three caves where you will see gold and silver stored. Do not touch it. You will then pass through a garden full of wonderful fruit and beyond the trees you will find a lamp. Pour out the oil and bring the lamp to me. Pick some of the fruit on your return if you wish."

Aladdin lifted the stone and saw some steps leading down into a cave. He was frightened to go down but the stranger placed a gold ring with a great green emerald on his finger.

"Take this ring as a gift," he said, "but you must go or I shall not buy you a shop."

Now the stranger was in fact a magician. He had read about a lamp with magical powers and he had traveled far to find it. He knew the magic would not work for him unless the lamp was fetched from the cavern and handed to him by someone else. After Aladdin had brought him the lamp the magician planned to shut him in the cave to die.

Down in the cavern Aladdin found all as he had been told. He hurried through the rooms filled with silver and gold, and passed through the garden where the trees were hung with shimmering fruit of all colors. At the far end stood an old lamp. Aladdin took it, poured out the oil, and then picked some of the

dazzling fruit from the trees as the magician had suggested. To his surprise they were all made from stones. Aladdin took as many as he could carry and returned to the steps.

"Give me the lamp," demanded the magician as soon as Aladdin came into sight.

"Help me out first," replied Aladdin who could not hand him the lamp because his arms were so full. They argued fiercely until *crash*, the stone slab fell back into place. The magician could not move the stone from the outside, nor Aladdin from within. He was trapped. The magician knew he had failed in his quest and decided to leave the country at once.

For two days Aladdin tried to get out of the cave. He became weak with hunger and thirst and finally as he sat in despair he rubbed his hands together. By chance he rubbed the gold ring that the stranger had given him. There was a blinding flash and a genie appeared. "I am the genie of the ring. What can I do for you, master?" it said.

"Get me out of here," Aladdin gasped. He was terrified of the great burning spirit of the genie glowing in the cavern. Before he knew what had happened he was standing on the ground above the entrance to the cavern. Of the stone slab there was no sign. Aladdin set off for home and collapsed with hunger as he entered the house.

His mother was overjoyed to see him. She gave him all the scraps of food she had and when she said she had no more Aladdin suggested selling the lamp to buy some food.

"I'll get a better price for it, if it's clean," she thought, and she rubbed the lamp with a cloth. In a flash the genie appeared. Aladdin's mother fainted in horror but Aladdin seized the lamp. When the genie saw him with the lamp it said:

"I am the genie of the lamp. What can I do for you, master?"

"Get me some food," ordered Aladdin.

By the time his mother had recovered there were twelve silver dishes of food and twelve silver cups on the table. Aladdin and his mother ate as they had never eaten before. They had enough for several days, and then Aladdin began to sell the silver dishes and cups. He and his mother lived comfortably in this way for some time.

Then it happened that Aladdin saw the sultan's daughter, Princess Badroulboudoir. Aladdin loved her at first sight and sent his mother to the sultan's court to ask the sultan's permission for the princess to marry him. He told her to take as a gift the stone fruits he had brought from the cave.

It was several days before Aladdin's mother could speak with the sultan, but at last she was able to give him the stone fruits. The sultan was truly amazed.

"Your son has such fine jewels he would make a good husband for my daughter, I am sure," he told Aladdin's mother.

But the sultan's chief courtier was jealous. He wanted his son to marry the princess. Quickly, he advised the sultan to say he would decide on the marriage in three months time. Aladdin was happy when he heard the news. He felt sure he would marry the princess in three months time.

But at the palace, the chief courtier spoke against Aladdin and when Aladdin's mother returned in three months, the sultan asked her:

"Can your son send me forty golden bowls full of jewels like the ones he sent before, only this time carried by forty servants?"

Aladdin rubbed the lamp once more and before long forty servants each carrying a gold bowl filled with sparkling jewels

were assembled in the courtyard of their little house.

When the sultan saw them, he said:

"I am sure now that the owner of these riches will make a fine husband for my daughter."

But the chief courtier suggested yet another test. "Ask the woman," he said, "if her son has a palace fit for your daughter to live in."

"I'll give him the land and he can build a new palace," declared the sultan, and he presented Aladdin with land in front of his own palace.

Aladdin summoned the genie of the lamp once more. Overnight the most amazing palace appeared with walls of gold and silver, huge windows, beautiful halls, and courtyards and rooms filled with treasures. A carpet of red velvet was laid from the old palace to the new, for the princess to walk on to her new home. Aladdin then asked the genie for some fine clothes for himself and his mother, and a glorious wedding took place with a splendid banquet eaten off golden dishes.

Aladdin took care always to keep the wonderful lamp safe. One day the princess gave it to an old beggar who was the magician in disguise, but that story, and the story of how Aladdin got it back again, will have to keep for another time.

The Three Bears

Robert Southey

There were once three bears who lived in a house of their own in the forest. There was a tiny baby bear, a middle-sized mother bear, and a great big father bear.

One morning their breakfast porridge was too hot to eat, so they decided to go for a walk in the forest. After they had gone, a little girl called Goldilocks came wandering along and noticed their house. She knocked on the door and, when nobody answered her, she pushed it open and went inside.

In front of her was a table with three chairs — one large chair, one middle-sized chair and one small chair. On the table were three bowls of porridge and three spoons — one large bowl and large spoon, one middle-sized bowl and middle-sized spoon, and one little bowl and little spoon.

Goldilocks was hungry after her walk in the forest and the porridge smelled good. She sat down in the great big chair, picked up the large spoon and tried some of the porridge from the large bowl. But the chair was far too big and too hard and the porridge was far too hot.

Goldilocks jumped down quickly and ran next to the middle-sized chair. But this chair was far too soft, and when she tried the porridge from the middle-sized bowl it was far too cold. So she went over to the little chair and tried some of the porridge from the little bowl. This time it was neither too hot nor too cold. It was just right and tasted so good that she ate it all up. But Goldilocks was too heavy for the little chair and it broke into pieces under her.

Goldilocks was feeling rather tired so she went upstairs where she found three beds. There was a great big bed, a middle-sized bed, and a tiny little bed. She climbed onto the big bed to have a nap but it was too hard and much too big. She tried the middle-sized bed but that was too soft so she jumped into the tiny little bed. It was not too hard and not too soft. It was just right and so cozy and warm that Goldilocks fell asleep as soon as her head touched the pillow.

After a short time, the three bears returned from their walk in the forest. They saw at once that somebody had opened wide the door of their house and gone inside. Father Bear looked around, then roared in a great big growly voice:

"SOMEBODY HAS BEEN SITTING IN MY CHAIR!"

Mother Bear said in a quiet gentle voice:

"Somebody has been sitting in my chair."

Then Baby Bear said in a small squeaky voice:

"*Somebody has been sitting in my chair, and has broken it.*"

Father Bear looked down at the table and saw the spoon still standing in his porridge. "SOMEBODY HAS BEEN EATING MY PORRIDGE," he roared in his great big growly voice.

Mother Bear saw her bowl with a spoon in it too. "Somebody has been eating my porridge," she said in her quiet gentle voice.

Baby Bear looked at his porridge bowl and said in his small squeaky voice, "*Somebody has been eating my porridge and has eaten it all up.*"

Then the three bears went upstairs to see if there was any more damage, and Father Bear saw at once that his bed was untidy. "SOMEBODY HAS BEEN SLEEPING IN MY BED," he said in his great big growly voice.

Mother Bear saw that the blankets on her bed were also untidy. "Somebody has been sleeping in my bed," she said in her quiet gentle voice.

Then Baby Bear looked at his bed and said in his small squeaky voice:

"*Somebody is sleeping in my bed – RIGHT NOW!*"

He squeaked so loudly that Goldilocks woke up with a start. She jumped out of the bed and down the stairs she ran, through the door and out into the forest. And the three bears never saw her again.

The Dragon and the Monkey

Traditional Chinese

Far away in the China Seas lived a dragon and his wife. She was fretful and rather difficult, but he was a kind and loving dragon. As they swam in the warm seas together she was forever complaining and asking her husband to fetch her different foods. He always thought, "This time I will really make her happy, and then how easy and lovely life will be." Yet somehow, whatever delicacy he fetched her, she was never satisfied and always wanted something else.

One day she twitched her tail more than usual, and told her husband that she was not feeling well and that she had heard a monkey's heart was the only thing to cure her.

"You are certainly looking pale, my love," said the dragon, "and you know I would do anything for you, but how can I possibly find you a monkey's heart? Monkeys live up trees, and I could never catch one."

"Now I know you don't love me." cried his wife. "If you did you would find a way to catch one. Now I shall surely die!"

The dragon sighed and swam off across the seas to an island where he knew some monkeys lived. "Somehow," he thought desperately, "I must trick a monkey into coming with me."

When he reached the island, he saw a little monkey sitting in a tree. The dragon called out:

"Hello monkey! It's good to see you! Come down and talk to me. That tree looks so unsafe, you might fall out!"

At that the monkey roared with laughter. "Ha! Ha! Ha! You are funny, dragon. Whoever heard of a monkey falling out of a tree?"

The dragon thought of his wife and tried again.

"I'll show you a tree covered with delicious juicy fruit, monkey. It grows on the other side of the sea."

Again the monkey laughed. "Ha! Ha! Ha! Whoever heard of a monkey swimming across the sea, dragon?"

"I could take you on my back, little monkey," said the dragon.

The monkey liked this idea and swung out of the tree onto the dragon's back. As he swam across the sea, the dragon thought there was no way the monkey could escape, so he said:

"I am sorry, little monkey, I've tricked you. There are no trees with delicious fruit where we are going. I am taking you to my wife who wishes to eat your heart. She says it is the only thing that will cure her of her illness."

The monkey looked at the water all around him and saw no way to escape, but he thought quickly, and said:

"Your poor wife! I am sorry to hear she's not well. There is nothing I'd like more than to give her my heart. But what a pity you did not tell me before we left. You obviously do not know, dragon, that we monkeys never carry our hearts with us. I left it behind in the tree where you found me. If you would be kind enough to swim back there with me, I shall willingly fetch it."

So the dragon turned around and swam back to the place where he had found the monkey. With one leap the monkey was in the branches of the tree, safe out of the dragon's reach.

"I'm sorry to disappoint you, dragon," he called out, "but I had my heart with me all the time. You won't trick me out of this tree again. Ha! Ha! Ha!"

There was no way the dragon could reach him and whether or not he ever caught another monkey I do not know. Perhaps he is still looking while his wife swims alone in the China Seas.

The Little Jackal

Traditional African

There was once a little jackal who lived in the jungle. He was a greedy little jackal, and one of his favorite meals was fresh crabs from the river. One day he went down to the big river near his home and put his paw in the water to pull out a crab.

Snap! A large, lazy crocodile who had been lying in the water snapped his jaws and caught the jackal's paw. The little jackal did not cry out, although he was very frightened. Instead he laughed.

"Ha! Ha! That crocodile in the river thinks he has caught my paw, but the stupid animal does not realize he has snapped up a piece of wood and is holding it in his jaws."

The crocodile immediately opened his mouth for he did not want to be seen with a log of wood in his jaws. Quickly the little jackal danced away and called cheekily from a safe distance:

"I'll catch some crabs another day, Mr. Crocodile."

The crocodile lashed his tail with rage and resolved to catch the little jackal and eat him the next time he came to the river.

A week later, when his paw was healed, the jackal came back to the river to catch crabs. He did not want to be eaten by the crocodile, so he called out from a safe distance:

"I can't see any crabs lying on the bank. I'll have to dip my paw into the water near the edge," and he watched the river for a few minutes.

The crocodile thought, "Now is my chance to catch the jackal," and he swam close to the river bank.

When the little jackal saw the water move, he called out:

"Thank you, Mr. Crocodile. Now I know you are there, I'll come back another day."

The crocodile lashed his tail with rage until he stirred up the mud from the bottom of the river. He swore he would not let the little jackal trick him again.

The jackal could not stop thinking about the crabs, so a few days later he went down to the river again. He could not see the crocodile so he called out:

"I know crabs make bubbles in the water, so as soon as I see bubbles I'll dip my paw in and then I'll catch them easily."

When he heard this, the crocodile, who was lying just beneath the water started to blow bubbles as fast as he could. He was sure that the jackal would put his paw in where the bubbles were rising and Snap! This time he would have the little jackal.

But when the jackal saw the bubbles, he called out:

"Thank you, Mr. Crocodile, for showing me where you are. I'll come back another day for the crabs."

The crocodile was so angry at being tricked again that he waited till the jackal's back was turned, then he jumped out of the river and followed the jackal, determined to catch him and eat him this time.

Now the jackal, who was very hungry, made his way to the fig grove to eat some figs. By the time the crocodile arrived, he was having a lovely feast munching the ripe blue fruit, and licking his lips with pleasure.

The crocodile was exhausted by walking on land which he found was much more difficult than swimming in the river. "I am too tired to catch the jackal now," he said to himself. "But I'll set a trap and catch him next time he comes for the figs."

The next day, the greedy jackal returned to the fig grove. He did love eating figs! To his surprise he saw a large and rather untidy pile of figs that had not been there before. "I wonder if my friend the crocodile has anything to do with this?" he said to himself, and he called out:

"What a lovely pile of figs! All I need to do is to see which figs wave in the breeze, for it is always the ripest and most delicious figs that wave in the breeze. I shall then know which ones to eat."

Of course the crocodile was buried under the pile of figs and when he heard this he smiled a big toothy crocodile smile. "All I have to do is to wriggle a bit," he thought. "When the jackal sees the figs move he will come and eat them and this time I will certainly catch him."

The little jackal watched as the crocodile wriggled under the pile of figs, and he laughed and laughed.

"Thank you, Mr. Crocodile," he said, "I'll come back another day when you are not here."

Now the crocodile was really in a rage so he followed the little jackal to his house to catch him there. There was no one at home when the crocodile got there, but the crocodile thought, "I will wait here, and catch him when he comes home tonight."

He was too big to go through the gate, so he broke it and then he was too big to go through the door, so he smashed that. "Never mind," he said to himself. "I will eat the little jackal tonight whatever happens," and he lay in wait for the jackal in the jackal's little house.

When the jackal came home he saw the broken gate, and smashed door, and he said to himself, "I wonder if my friend the crocodile has anything to do with this?"

"Little house," he called out, "why haven't you said 'hello' to me as you do each night when I come home?"

The crocodile heard this, and thought he ought to make everything seem as normal as possible, so he shouted out:

"Hello little jackal!"

Then a wicked smile appeared on the jackal's face. He fetched some twigs and branches, piled them up outside his house, and set fire to it. As the house burned he called out:

"A roast crocodile is safer than a live crocodile! I shall go and build myself a new house by the river where I can catch all the crabs I want."

With that he skipped off to the river bank and for all I know he is still there today, eating crabs all day long, and laughing at the way he tricked the crocodile.

The Tinder Box

Hans Christian Andersen

A soldier was marching along the road on his way home from the wars one day when an old woman came out from behind a tree and stopped him. She was as ugly as a witch but she seemed friendly enough as she admired the soldier's sword.

"How would you like to take home with you as much money as you can carry, soldier?" she asked.

"I'd like it a lot," he said, "only where can I find the money, old woman?"

"Listen and I'll tell you," the witch woman replied. "If you climb into this tree, you will find it is hollow. Go down inside it and you will find yourself in a deep shaft. At the bottom there is a passage and you will see three doors.

"The first door leads to a room guarded by a fierce dog with eyes as big as tea cups. In it you will find as much bronze money as you could want. Take this apron of mine and spread it out on the floor. If the dog sits on it he will do you no harm. But if you prefer it, go on to the second door."

"What shall I find there?" interrupted the soldier.

"Ah!" said the old woman. "There you will find as much silver as you can carry, and more. But this room is guarded by a dog whose eyes are as big as mill wheels. He too is fierce, but will not hurt you once he has sat on my apron.

"In the last room you will find gold coins, masses and masses of gold coins, but take care here, for the dog that guards the gold has eyes as big as towers. He is even fiercer, but he too will not hurt you if he sits on my apron."

"It all sounds very good, old woman," said the soldier cheerfully, "but what are you going to get out of it? I can't believe you would give me this chance to get rich without wanting a favor of some kind yourself."

"Quite right, soldier," she replied. "You must bring me the tinder box that lies on the table at the end of the passage. My grandmother gave it to me, but I forgot to bring it up last time I was down there. I'm too old now to climb down the shaft to fetch it. Tie this rope around your waist so that I can help pull you up when you have finished."

The soldier tied the rope around his waist and climbed into the hollow tree. It was just as the old woman had described and the soldier clambered down a long shaft deep into the ground, and found himself in a passage. It was lit by many candles so he could see the three doors quite clearly.

He opened the first door and gasped with pleasure. There before him were chests and chests of bronze money but standing in front of them was a fierce-looking dog with eyes as big as tea cups. The soldier whistled cheerfully and laid the apron on the floor.

To his relief the dog sat on the apron and the soldier went over to the chests and stuffed his pockets with the bronze money. Then he picked up the apron and returned to the passage.

The soldier went on to the second door, and when he peeped inside he saw an even fiercer dog with eyes as big as mill wheels. Behind him were caskets full of silver. The greedy soldier put the witch's apron on the ground and as soon as the dog was sitting on it, he emptied all the bronze money out of his pockets, picked up handfuls of silver coins and filled his pockets and his knapsack. He was so weighed down when he left the room he could scarcely pick up the witch's apron. He then staggered on down the passage to the third door.

Inside, the whole room seemed to sparkle from the gold the soldier could see, but between him and the gold stood the fiercest-looking dog he had ever seen with eyes as big as towers. The soldier spread the apron on the floor very carefully and to his relief the dog sat on it. The soldier quickly threw out all the silver he had collected, and picked up gold coins as fast as he could, cramming them into his pockets, his knapsack and even his hat.

The soldier went back to the shaft to climb up into the hollow tree. He tugged at the rope so the old woman could help him, but she called down:

"Did you get my tinder box, soldier?"

"Why no, I forgot!" called back the soldier. "I'll get it now."

He went back along the passage and found the tinder box where she had said it would be, and he picked it up and returned to the bottom of the shaft.

As soon as he was out of the hollow tree the soldier asked the old woman why the tinder box was so important to her but she would not tell him. "If you don't answer me," he shouted, "I shall cut off your head with my fine sword," but the old woman just held out her hand for the tinder box. The soldier, who was used to getting his own way, drew his sword and with one swift stroke he chopped off her head.

The soldier went on his way cheerfully, and in the evening he came to a big town and took rooms in the best inn. The innkeeper was surprised that a mere soldier wanted such an expensive room, and the boot boy wondered at the shabby old boots put out to be cleaned, but they said nothing, for they had seen the gleam of gold in the soldier's hand.

The next day, the soldier went out and bought himself fine clothes and new boots. For many months he stayed in the inn, and lived like a rich gentleman. He made many friends and gave wild expensive parties. Each day his supply of gold got less until the day came when he had nothing at all.

Now the soldier had to move into a small dismal attic room. His new friends disappeared and the soldier found himself alone and cold and hungry. One dark night as he sat huddled in a chair he caught sight of an old candle stub. It was all he had left to give him a few moments of warmth and light. Remembering the old woman's tinder box, he struck it once to light the candle. To his amazement he saw the dog with eyes as big as tea cups in the room with him.

"What do you want, master?" the dog asked. "Shall I fetch you some money?" and even as the soldier nodded the dog disappeared and returned with a bag of bronze coins in his mouth.

The soldier struck the tinder box twice and the dog with eyes as big as mill wheels was there, saying, "What do you want, master?" and he too disappeared and came back with a bag of money, but this time it was in silver coins. The soldier struck the tinder box again three times, and there was the huge dog with eyes as big as towers. In a flash, he too disappeared and returned with a bag of gold coins.

"Now I know why the old woman was so anxious to get this tinder box," said the soldier, smiling to himself.

The next day he moved to fine lodgings and all his friends came to see him again, and the parties started once more. The soldier seemed to have everything he could want, but there was one thing he could not do, and this annoyed him very much. At the end of the town was the king's palace, and it was said the king had a most beautiful daughter. The soldier longed to see her but his friends told him it was impossible.

"No one is allowed to see her," they said. "The king was once told that she would marry a common soldier so now he keeps her in the palace where she will never meet anyone but a prince."

The soldier often thought about the princess and wondered how he could arrange to see her. One night he had an idea. He struck the tinder box once and when the dog with eyes as big as tea cups appeared, he did not ask for money as he usually did, but told the dog he wished to see the princess. In no time at all the dog

returned carrying the sleeping princess on its back. The soldier found her extremely beautiful and made up his mind that each night one of the dogs should bring the princess to him.

One morning the princess told her parents of a dream she often had. "It is a strange dream," she said. "A huge dog with enormous eyes appears and carries me into the town and then to a room where there is a fine rich gentleman."

The king and queen were worried and asked one of the ladies-in-waiting to watch the princess during the night. That night the lady-in-waiting kept watch and saw a great dog with eyes as big as mill wheels carry the princess away on its back. Quickly she followed them through the town to the house where the dog took the princess. Then she made a cross on the door with chalk. But the dog saw her and, after he had returned the princess to the palace, he put chalk crosses on all the doors in the town.

The next day the king and queen, led by the lady-in-waiting, set out to find the scoundrel who sent his dog each night to fetch their daughter, but as they found each door marked with a cross

they were completely confused. The queen was determined to find out what happened to their daughter each night, so she made another plan. She filled a little silk bag with fine flour, snipped a small hole in the corner and tied this to her daughter before she went to bed.

The next morning she and the king were able to follow the trail of flour to the soldier's lodgings. Immediately the king had the soldier thrown into prison, and announced that he would be executed the next day.

As the soldier sat in his cell waiting for death, a boy outside tripped and lost his shoe through the cell grating. "If you want it back," called the soldier, "go to my lodgings and bring me my tinder box. I'll give you four pence too." The boy went willingly to fetch the tinder box for he was glad to earn four pence.

A large crowd gathered to see the soldier executed. As he climbed the scaffold the soldier asked for one last wish.

"Let me smoke my pipe one last time before I die," he said.

"Very well, soldier," said the king. "Your wish is granted."

The soldier took out his tinder box. He struck it once, then twice, then three times.

Immediately the three huge dogs appeared and their master shouted, "Save me!"

The dogs bounded forward and the king and queen and all the guards were slain. Most of the crowd ran away, but those who stayed decided that the soldier should be their new king. They could see he was very powerful!

The soldier gladly accepted and the first thing he did was to marry the beautiful princess. They lived together in the palace and the soldier always had everything he wanted, for the dog with eyes as big as tea cups, the dog with eyes as big as mill wheels and the dog with eyes as big as towers were always there to carry out his orders. And from that day onward, the soldier was careful to carry the tinder box with him wherever he went.

Puss-in-Boots

Charles Perrault

Amiller once died, leaving his three sons all that he possessed — his mill, his donkey, and his cat. They quickly arranged between them that the eldest son should keep the mill, the middle son the donkey, while the youngest should take the cat.

"It is very hard on me," grumbled the youngest son. "My brothers can earn their living with the mill and the donkey, but once I have eaten the cat, I will have nothing."

"Don't talk like that, master," said the cat. "Give me some boots and a sack with a string to tie at the top and you shall see that it was a lucky day for you when you became my master."

The cat quickly went to catch some mice and rats to prove how useful he was, and the miller's son found him the boots and a sack which tied at the top. The cat pulled on the boots and strutted around proudly. Then, taking the sack, he filled it with bran and tempting green leaves and set out for a nearby field where he knew there were rabbits. There he lay down with the sack open beside him and pretended to sleep.

Before long some curious rabbits came to investigate the sleeping cat and the sack, and when they smelled the delicious food they hopped into the sack. In a flash Puss-in-Boots jumped up, pulled the string tight, and caught the rabbits.

Now he strode off to the king's palace and demanded to see the king. "I have a gift for him from my master, the Marquis of Carabas," he announced. This was a name he had made up for the miller's son to impress the king.

"Thank your master for me," said the king, "and tell him I am pleased with his gift."

Some time later Puss-in-Boots set out again with his sack. This time he put a handful of corn in the sack and caught some partridge, and once more he took them to the king's palace, and presented them to the king from the Marquis of Carabas.

Not long afterward Puss-in-Boots heard that the King was going to drive with his daughter by the river, and he told the miller's son to follow him and do whatever he said. By now the lad realized that Puss was no ordinary cat, and he promised to do everything he was told.

Puss then asked the miller's son to take off his clothes and swim in the river. When the king's carriage came past he called out, "Help! My master, the Marquis of Carabas, is drowning!"

The king, hearing the name of the Marquis, stopped his carriage, and ordered his guards to save the young man. While they were dragging him out, the cat told the king that robbers had run off with his master's clothes. The truth was that Puss had hidden the clothes under a stone. Quickly the king sent one of his servants to fetch some fine clothes, for he remembered the gifts of game Puss had brought to the palace.

When the miller's son put on the new clothes he looked very handsome indeed. The king's daughter immediately fell in love with him, and the king invited him to drive with them.

Puss ran on ahead and found some men working in a field. "The king is about to drive past," he told them. "If he asks you who owns this field, you must answer 'The Marquis of Carabas'. If you don't," he added, "you shall be chopped into little pieces."

A few moments later the king's carriage came along and the king asked the men who owned the land. They remembered the fierce threats from Puss-in-Boots and answered:

"The Marquis of Carabas, Sire."

The king was impressed. Again the cat ran ahead and found some harvesters cutting corn. He told them to say all the fields they were working in belonged to the Marquis of Carabas. If they did not, he said he would make sure they were killed. When the king heard that the Marquis of Carabas owned this land too he was even more impressed.

107

Meanwhile Puss hurried on to a big castle where a wicked magician lived. The magician was the real owner of the land through which the king and his companions were driving.

The cat knocked at the door and asked to see the magician, and when he met him he bowed very low. "Is it true that you can change yourself into any animal – a lion, a tiger, even an elephant?" he asked with great respect.

"It is true," replied the magician and turned into a great lion. Puss-in-Boots was terrified and only just managed to scramble to safety on a roof – not easy for a cat wearing big boots. There he huddled until the lion changed back into the magician.

"That was truly remarkable," he said to the magician most politely. "But I don't suppose you can also turn yourself into a tiny animal like a mouse or a rat?"

"That's even easier," said the magician, and in a flash he became a tiny mouse, scampering on the floor. With a leap Puss pounced on him and that was the end of the magician.

Just then Puss-in-Boots heard the king's carriage arriving at the castle. He ran outside and said to the king, "Welcome to the house of my master, the Marquis of Carabas."

The king entered with his daughter and the miller's son and looked around the fine castle. Realizing that his daughter already loved the young man, he said, "Tell me, Marquis, what would you say to marrying my daughter?"

The miller's son, who had fallen deeply in love with the princess, bowed very low and accepted. That very same day he married the princess, and you may be sure Puss-in-Boots was always well fed and well looked after for the rest of his life.

Henny Penny

Traditional

One day Henny Penny was scratching in the farmyard looking for something good to eat when, suddenly, something hit her on the head. "My goodness me!" she said. "The sky must be falling down. I must go and tell the king."

She had not gone far when she met her friend Cocky Locky, and he called out, "Where are you going in such a hurry?"

"I am going to tell the king that the sky is falling down," said Henny Penny.

"I will come with you," said Cocky Locky.

So Henny Penny and Cocky Locky hurried along together toward the king's palace. On the way they saw Ducky Lucky swimming on the pond. "Where are you going?" he called out.

"We are going to tell the king the sky is falling down," replied Henny Penny. "We must go quickly, as there is no time to lose."

"I will come with you," said Ducky Lucky.

So Henny Penny, Cocky Locky, and Ducky Lucky hurried on together toward the king's palace. On the way they met Goosey Loosey, who called out, "Where are you all going in such a hurry?"

"We are on our way to tell the king the sky is falling down," said Henny Penny.

"I will come with you," said Goosey Loosey.

So Henny Penny, Cocky Locky, Ducky Lucky, and Goosey Loosey hurried on together toward the king's palace.

Around the next corner they met Turkey Lurkey. "Where are you all going on this fine day?" she called out to them.

"It won't be a fine day for long," replied Henny Penny. "The sky is falling down, and we are hurrying to tell the king."

"I will come with you," said Turkey Lurkey.

So Henny Penny, Cocky Locky, Ducky Lucky, Goosey Loosey, and Turkey Lurkey went on together toward the king's palace.

Now on their way they met Foxy Loxy who asked, "Where are you going in such a hurry?"

"We are going to the king's palace to tell him the sky is falling down," replied Henny Penny.

"That is a very important message," said Foxy Loxy. "I will come with you. In fact if you follow me I can show you a short cut to the king's palace, so we will get there sooner."

So Henny Penny, Cocky Locky, Ducky Lucky, Goosey Loosey,

and Turkey Lurkey all followed Foxy Loxy. He led them to the wood, and up to a dark hole, which was the door to his home. Inside his wife and five hungry children were waiting for him to bring home some dinner.

That, I am sorry to say, was the end of Cocky Locky, Ducky Lucky, Goosey Loosey, and Turkey Lurkey, for one by one they all followed Foxy Loxy into his home, and they were all eaten up by the hungry fox family.

Henny Penny was the last to enter the Fox's hole and she heard Cocky Locky crowing in alarm in front of her. Squawking with fright and scattering feathers, she turned and ran as fast as she could for the safety of her own farmyard. There she stayed and she never did tell the king that the sky was falling down.

The Little Red Hen and the Fox

Traditional Irish and American

A little red hen lived all alone in a house in the forest. She was a houseproud little hen who always kept her house neat and tidy. She always wore an apron and in the pocket she kept scissors and a needle and thread, for she always said, "You never know when they will come in handy."

Now the little red hen had one enemy — a rascally fox who lived over the hill. The fox used to lie awake at night thinking how much he would enjoy eating the little red hen. But the little red hen took great care not to fall into any of the fox's traps when she was out in the forest, and in the evening she always stayed at home. What is more, she always locked her door when she went out and slipped the key into her pocket with the scissors and needle and thread, so that the greedy fox could not creep into her house and surprise her when she came home. She locked the door behind her too, whenever she was inside the house.

The fox used to watch her from behind a tree, and one day he said to his old mother who lived with him, "Mother! Stoke up the fire, and keep a big pot boiling, for tonight I am going to catch the little red hen. I have worked out a plan which will not fail."

The fox took a sack, slung it over his shoulder, and set out over the hill to catch the little red hen. He crept as close as he could to the little red hen's house, and there he lay in wait.

Sure enough, before he had been there an hour, the little red hen came out.

She was just going to the wood pile to bring in some wood, so she did not bother to lock the door behind her. Quick as a flash that old rascal the fox was inside her house with his sack, and was waiting for her as she returned with some sticks.

"Hello there, little red hen," he called out as she shut the door. "I have caught you now, and you are coming home with me for my supper!"

With a flurry of feathers and a great deal of squawking, the little red hen flew out of the fox's reach, and settled on the rafters above his head.

"Don't you be so sure of yourself, you old rascal," said the little red hen. "You can't reach me up here."

That was true. The fox sat down wondering what to do next, and all the while the little red hen sat up in the rafters hoping the fox would get bored or hungry and go and look for his supper elsewhere. But foxes are not called cunning for nothing, and the

old rascal soon had a plan. He started to twirl and turn, around and around, chasing his own tail. Faster and faster he went until the whole house seemed to be full of twirling red fox.

The little red hen grew so dizzy watching him spin that she lost her balance and fell off her rafter with a great thud. In a trice the fox bundled her into his sack, flung it over his shoulder and set out over the hill to his home.

At first, the little red hen was confused by her dizziness and the fall, and by the darkness in the sack, but her mind soon cleared, and she lay quietly waiting for a chance to escape.

The fox, even though he had succeeded in bringing the little red hen down off the rafters, was still feeling quite dizzy and breathless from all that spinning around. So on the way home he sat down for a rest and put the sack on the ground beside him. In no time at all, the little red hen had taken her scissors from her pocket and snip, snip, snip, she cut her way out of the sack. She saw a stone nearby and rolled it into the sack and, while the fox was lying back chuckling to himself, that little red hen stitched up the hole. She finished sewing and just had time to hide behind a tree before the fox took up the sack once more and hurried on over the hill to his own house.

"Here I am, mother," he called, as he came into his house. "Is the pot boiling? The little red hen is in the sack."

"Everything is ready," replied his mother. "Put the hen straight into the boiling water."

"Here she comes," said the fox, as he opened the sack and emptied it into the cooking pot.

Splash! The stone fell into the water.

"That's a very odd hen," shrieked the fox's mother. "How dare you fool me like that!" But the fox knew that it was he who had been fooled by the little red hen.

He and his mother went to bed hungry that night, and the next day the fox went hunting for his supper elsewhere. As for the little red hen, she went home and, for the rest of her days, she always carried a pair of scissors and a needle and thread in her pocket, and she would always say with a smile, "You never know when they will come in handy."

The Traveling Musicians

Grimm Brothers

One day an old donkey overheard his master saying that he was too old for work. The time had come for him to be killed off for they could not keep an animal who was no longer useful.

"Killed indeed!" snorted the donkey. "I may be too old to carry heavy loads but I am not too old to make a fine noise when I bray. I shall go to the neighboring town of Bremen and earn my keep there as a musician."

He unlatched the stable door with his teeth, a trick he had learned long ago, and when no one was looking he slipped out and trotted down the road toward Bremen.

He had not gone far when he saw an old dog lying by the side of the road looking rather sorry for himself.

"Why so sad, Dog?" he asked.

"You would feel just as sad if you had overheard your master say he was going to knock you on the head because you were too old."

"Come with me, friend," said the donkey. "I am also too old for my master, so I am off to Bremen to earn my living as a musician. You can use your voice, can't you? Together we will sing a fine duet."

The dog agreed to travel to Bremen with the donkey, and they trotted down the road together. Before long, they saw a cat hunched up and miserable sitting on a gate.

"It's a fine day, Cat," they said, "far too fine for you to look so sad."

"It's a bad sad day for me," said the cat. "My owners say I no longer catch as many rats and mice as I did when I was young, so they are replacing me with a kitten. They cannot feed us both, so I am going to be put in a sack and drowned in the river."

"Don't wait for that to happen," said the donkey and the dog. "We are also too old for our masters, but we have not waited to be finished off. We are on our way to Bremen to earn our living as musicians. You still have your voice. Come with us."

The cat uttered a fine "Meow!" in agreement.

So the three animals journeyed on to Bremen together. At the next farm they met a cock strutting up and down. All his feathers were ruffled out in indignation.

"What's the trouble, Cock?" they asked. "You look upset."

"How would you feel," replied the cock, "if you overheard your mistress planning to wring your neck so she could cook you for dinner on Sunday when they have visitors coming?"

"Come with us to Bremen," said the donkey, the dog and the cat. "We are going to earn our living there as musicians. We're sure you have a fine singing voice."

"Indeed I do," said the cock, and to show them he uttered a loud "Cock-a-doodle-doo!"

It was too far for them to reach Bremen that day, so when evening came they found a sheltered place in a wood to rest for the night. The dog and the donkey settled themselves comfortably at the bottom of a tree, the cat climbed into the branches, and the cock roosted high up at the top. They were all tired, but none of them slept for they were all so hungry.

When it was quite dark the animals saw a light shining from a house they had not noticed before. It made them think of food, and the cat said, "Friends, let's go and investigate. Where there is a house, there may be something to eat."

Together they crept up to one of the windows where a light was shining. The donkey being the tallest looked through first.

"Well, friend, what do you see?" asked the cock.

"I see a table laden with food and drink, and a group of mean-looking men counting piles of money," said the donkey.

The cat, the dog, and the cockerel jumped up onto the donkey's back and peered through the window too. They did not realize it but they had discovered a robbers' hideout.

"Let us try out our music," said one of the animals. "If we sing a fine song for them they may give us some of their supper."

Together they all sang. The donkey brayed, the dog barked, the cat yowled and the cock crowed. The noise was tremendous.

The effect was not at all what they expected, for the robbers, hearing this noise, thought they were about to be arrested. They ran helter-skelter as fast as they could into the woods, leaving the doors wide open.

"That was nice of them," said the four animals, when the robbers did not reappear. "They have gone away and left us their home to enjoy."

The donkey found some good hay in the barn and the cock some grain, while the cat and the dog ate all they wanted from the robbers' table. Then they all slept soundly. In time the candles burned down and went out and the house lay in darkness.

Some hours later, the robbers returned. They had been arguing among themselves, for some thought they had given in too easily by running away without a fight, while the others thought it was foolish to go back to the house, for they would surely be caught and put in prison. Now they drew nearer, and seeing no sign of life they decided it would be safe for one of them to return and take some of the gold they had left behind.

Quietly the robber crept up to the house, and tried to light a candle. As he did so the cat awoke, and the robber saw his green eyes glowing in the dark. Mistaking them for the embers of the fire, he held a splinter of wood to them.

The cat, thinking he was being attacked, flew at the robber, spitting and scratching for all he was worth. The robber, fearing some great wild beast was attacking him, dropped the wood and ran for his life. In the doorway he tripped over the dog who howled and bit the robber's ankle. The robber limped across the yard where the donkey lashed out at him with his heels. Then the cock, hearing all the commotion and fearing his friends were being killed, flew at the robber with his claws.

The robber fled back to his companions. "It is surely a monster and a devil rolled into one that has taken over our house," he said. "First I was scratched, then bitten, then kicked, and finally attacked from above by fierce talons and whirling feathers. The noise of screeching and howling was enough to wake the dead. We must never go back there again."

So it was that the robbers set off for another part of the country and left their hideout in the woods to the animals. In the morning the four musicians discussed the odd disturbances in the middle of the night. Since the stranger had disappeared they decided to stay where they were for a time.

"We will go to Bremen another day," they said.

But they never did go to Bremen. Instead they lived happily in the house for many years and never tried singing together again.

The Great Flood

Traditional Bible and Fable

Long, long ago in a far off land there was a great flood. For days and weeks and months it rained and rained and rained. Puddles turned into lakes and tiny streams into great rivers and in time the whole earth was covered with water. This is the story of how it happened.

At that time wicked people lived on the earth. They lived violent, evil lives. God saw this and was deeply hurt.

"I am sorry that I ever made the human race," God said. "I will end the whole dreadful business. I will destroy the people, the animals, the reptiles, the wild birds – everything."

But there was one family who made God pause for a moment. "Noah and his family," thought God. "No! I cannot destroy them. They are good people and love me. I know what I shall do."

Now Noah was a very old man and he and his wife had three sons called Shem, Ham, and Japheth, all of whom were married. One day Noah was working in the fields when God appeared to him.

"Build a ship on dry land," God commanded him. "Build it high and broad and long. Make windows in it and a strong door in the side and build it with three decks, each divided into many compartments. Seal it, too, inside and out with pitch and keep it watertight.

"When the time comes, take into this great ark pairs of every animal – reptiles and birds as well – and enough food to feed them all. For I am going to send a flood of water over the whole land. I will destroy everything that lives except you and your family and the creatures with you in the ark."

Noah and his sons began to build the ark as God commanded them. For months they sawed down trees, cut them into planks and hammered them into place. The people who lived around them stared in amazement as the huge ship began to take shape, and laughed at them for working so hard. "Where are you going to sail that?" they jeered. "It's wider than the river."

But Noah and his sons worked on and at last the ship was ready. It had windows all around and a huge door on one side. Inside were three decks, each divided into different rooms. Some of these were filled with food of all kinds — flour and dried fruit, vegetables, grain, and stacks of hay. Whatever Noah and his family could find, they stored in the ark.

Now the time came when God told Noah to call the animals and to tell his family to enter the great ship. And now two by two the animals came. There were great cats and tiny mice and the smallest of insects. There were antelope and horses, camels and rhinoceroses, lizards, snakes, and tortoises.

It took seven days for them all to arrive and soon the ark was very full indeed. On the seventh day as heavy spots of rain splashed down God told Noah to enter and close the ark.

The clouds grew darker and the rain began to fall more and more heavily. Never before had such rain been seen. It poured like a waterfall from the sky and the seas began to rise. Huge tidal waves flowed over the land, drowning everything in their path. Day after day it rained until all that could be seen was the ark floating on a vast gray sea.

At last the rain fell more gently and slowly the flood began to go down. The animals and Noah's family lived together for five months without sight of anything but water. Now they felt their ship settle on solid ground. They had come to rest on the top of a mountain called Ararat.

Noah peered anxiously out of a window. He and his family and all the animals longed to be on land once more but only the mountain tops could be seen. Everywhere else was still covered with water and Noah did not dare to open the door.

After waiting a while he let a raven out to see if it could find somewhere to settle. It never came back and after a week Noah sent out a dove. The dove flew around but could find nowhere to rest or find food so it came back to the ark. When Noah saw it fluttering outside, he knew the earth must still be covered with water and he let the bird inside.

Another week he waited with all the animals. Then Noah sent out the dove again and this time it returned in the evening with an olive branch in its beak. Now Noah knew the waters were really going down. He waited one more week and again sent out the dove. When it did not return Noah knew it was time to leave the ark. He opened the door a crack and in every direction he saw green grass and trees and flowers.

Noah called his family together and all the animals grew quiet to listen to him.

"The time has come," he told them. "Now we can leave the ark." Then he and his sons pushed open the great door.

Out poured the animals, squawking and barking, neighing and roaring. Out scampered the mice; out ran the rabbits and hares; out leapt the zebras, the sheep and the horses; out stalked the bears too and the stately lions, while the birds sang and fluttered overhead. All the animals were glad to be out in the open once more with room to leap or fly or dance or just to curl up in the warm sunshine.

God saw the destruction he had caused and said to Noah:

"I will never again send such a flood. Never again will I destroy all living creatures or curse the land. And as a sign that I shall keep this promise, I give you the rainbow."

Just then a brilliant rainbow arched over the ark and over Noah and his family and all the animals. Ever since that day, whenever the sun comes out in the rain, you will see a rainbow in the sky. It reminds us of God's promise that there will never again be a great flood over the whole earth.